THE JAGUAR KING II

L. E. Zimmerman

BAD CREATIVE BOOKS

Did you know Leopards can run up to 58km/h? They can also leap 6m forward through the air. That's the length of three adults lying head to toe. Beastly.

This book is a work of fiction. Names, characters, places and incidents are products of the author's imagination or are used fictitiously. Any resemblance to actual events or locales or persons, living or dead, is entirely coincidental.

ISBN 9781952767357

OTHER BADCREATIVE BOOKS

The Jaguar King
Bewitching Amelia
Banking On Love

Table of Contents

Prologue – An Offer She Didn't Refuse

Chapter 1 – Vacation and Vocation

Chapter 2 – The Ideology Of Illusions

Chapter 3 – Back To School

Chapter 4 – The Next Move

Chapter 5 – Awakened Blood

Chapter 6 – Iron and Blood

Chapter 7 – Omen Of a Gathering

Chapter 8 – Into The Skies

Chapter 9 – Across Great Distances

Chapter 10 – Mr Viejas Test

Chapter 11 – Defeat and Revenge

Chapter 12 – Planning the Counterattack

Chapter 13 – Building an Army

Chapter 14 – The Spark of Hope

PROLOGUE

An Offer She Didn't Refuse

Four months had passed since Fiona Marois had taken up Mr. Viejas on his offer. She truly couldn't have refused it back then; a job to travel the world and build relations with people and places of interest that Mr. Viejas wanted? It was too golden of an opportunity to decline. Fiona ran her hands through her wavy blond hair, cut shorter for the summer season as she took in the sights around her. The sun was beginning to set behind the mountain that held the Kannonji temple. The sky was painted with an orange glow, and the sakura blossoms came alive with a vibrant pink color, giving the area a surreal effect. Yet, it was all so real as Fiona smiled at how beautiful the area she was in, was. Some of the buildings throughout the small town came to life, as the arcades beamed on their neon lights. Restaurants began to prepare dinner, as the salarymen got off work and started to pile into the bars and dinner joints for an evening meal and drink, with friends and coworkers. Taxis were coming and going, and the silver train with green painted along the side of it arrived at the station above Fiona, its tracks resting on elevated pillars of concrete that traveled above the town. The station also doubled as a small shopping area of sorts, where travelers could grab sweet confectionaries, sushi in bento boxes, groceries, beauty products, manga, or drinks to start. Cars and people were walking about the street in a rather orderly fashion, passing through with little noise or talking. The buildings arounds were all compact compared to those in Canada, all the signs written in kanji. The scent of spices and meats wafted through one of the buildings, which Fiona happily inhaled and savored. Her senses were much more heightened than the usual human, for it was revealed to her by Mr. Viejas and Rodrigo that she had an innate ability within, one that made her more attuned to her own basic instincts. Fiona at first been immensely skeptical, that is until Mr. Viejas had shown her with a set of enchanted stones. Fiona had concentrated hard on seeing a leopard in her mind, which in turn led to seeing the actual ghostly apparition of one appear before her. Realizing that, along with her awareness, reflexes and senses all matching with what she was told, Fiona took a second look at the fact that she indeed had the spirit of something with her. Taking in the life and scenery around her, Fiona decided she wanted to go pay the temple a visit and started walking across a bridge, over a river that led to the mountainside of the town. The air was warm but not uncomfortable, as Fiona was completely out of her element and had not a care in the world. Here she was in Japan, a place she had wanted to visit since she was young; she had made the dream come to life at last. An hour from Tokyo, Fiona was staying in the cozy town of Ōfuna in the Kanagawa Prefecture. The plastered white head of the bodhisattva Kannon loomed over the trees on the mountain, looking down with a peaceful face. It was an easy enough location marker to navigate to, as Fiona made her way through the area. The switch of scenery there was almost night and day with a simple crossing of the bridge. On the train station side was all the shops and buildings. On the side that Fiona crossed to, a small rural area that had houses resting on steep roads near the mountain. Up one of the roads to get there was a convenience store, as well as a vending machine for drinks. Fiona adored the vending machines there for she learned that the sheer exotic variety of drinks was wonderful to pick from, as well as the drinks either being served cold or hot. Fiona saw her resident spirit within appear next to her, a golden transparent apparition of a woman with long hair and a headband floating next to her.

"Fiona, I can feel your spiritual awareness hiking up," she said to her.

"Is that bad, Sarita?" Fiona replied, curious but excited as she made her way up a street.

"Not at all. If anything, you seem to be in the presence of a great spiritual area. Are you heading to a sacred place of worship by any chance?"

"I am. I'm heading to the Kannonji temple to pay respects. I love visiting different churches and places of worship, for it helps broaden my own understanding of different cultures as well as gaining insight on the religion of a land," Fiona replied. The glow of Sarita started to become brighter and the outline of her details became clearer as she floated beside Fiona. While the two headed up the streets together, some of the people would look on at Fiona with startled faces. "Uh…I thought others couldn't see you, Sarita.

Can they see you here?" Fiona asked, the looks of the locals making her uneasy. "They can't. However, they must sense me with you. The people here must be very spiritually aware. Certainly not a bad thing," Sarita replied. "It's vital to maintain a connection with the side of the spirits. It takes inner peace and understanding to achieve such a thing."

"Sarita, I still don't know much about you," Fiona said, realizing her spirit companion was so knowledgeable yet divulged little about her own life. "I only began communing with you a month ago or so. Who were you when you were in the living world?"

"I was known as a druid medium. I often found myself in nature and in contact with other spirits and essences. What you have attached to you is my spirit and essence from so long ago."

"What are essences?" Fiona asked.

"Essences are the remnants of abilities and will manifested in a spirit-like state. As you've gleaned from Mr. Viejas, my tribe were all people who had an ability to shift into leopards at will," Sarita replied. "I'm the exception in terms of essences, for my own spirit is still here in this world." As the two made their way to the top of the hill, Fiona asked, "Why just you?"

"I anchored myself to this world before I met my end. There's another essence I wanted to meet again, that I knew would likely survive into these modern times. I don't know if it did, but I had to stay in this world in some capacity beyond my own essence."

"I see. Since you're a spirit as well, do you see other spirits?"

"I can indeed. Sarita replied. Where we're at right now has quite a few as we draw nearer to that temple." Fiona took a right and saw a stair set built into the mountainside that led up. A red banner and series of flags all hung along the stair set as Fiona looked up and saw the top of the Kannonji statue. "Sarita, I think we're almost there," she said as she began to make her way up the steps. A gentle wind blew through the mountain side as the grass and trees rustled. Fiona took a deep breath of the fragrant air and exhaled deeply, increasing her pace to get to the temple even faster. As the pair made their way up the main set of steps, there was a small kiosk with a woman in a kimono behind the desk. Fiona approached her and saw it was a place where one paid an admission fee of three hundred yen, as well as having the option to buy charms and talismans. Fiona deposited three of the silver coins marked "100" into the change can on the desk, as well as giving a few more and pointing to a red talisman in a seal. The woman in the kimono handed it to her, before nodding her thanks. Fiona did likewise and pocketed the talisman before moving to a fountain with a brass ladle. "What is this?" Sarita asked, further out of her element. Fiona, having studied Japanese culture, replied, "A place where you wash your hands. You use the ladle to pour into your hand and wash them. It's believed to help cleanse the spirit." Fiona then began her ascent up the next set of well decorated steps above. Arriving at the top, there was a wooden overpass gate with a *shimenawa* rope hung above it. Fiona was delightfully taking in all the sights, completely mesmerized with where she was at. Laid around were various stones and statues, each with kanji writing to explain what it was with an English translation below it. Behind a murky glass, a fire burned within a lantern, and on the table upon which it sat, the writing showed it was a flame to honor the fallen at Hiroshima. Fiona shivered at the sight as she walked up to it.

"What's the trouble?" Sarita asked Fiona, sensing her trepidation. "It's a lantern to honor those at Hiroshima. Hiroshima is a location in Japan that was bombed in 1945 and caused an egregious loss of life and destruction. To this day, it's still a grim reminder of the horrid reality of war," Fiona said.

"How terrible was the loss?"

"It was estimated at 140,000." Sarita's stoic eyes went wide as she asked, "How such a large death toll?"

"From a bomb. A bomb is an explosive device that is used in war. This one was made to destroy on a terribly powerful level," Fiona replied as she headed for the final stair set that lay ahead.

"That's awful. I know in my former tribe, we warred with others for survival and conquest. But such a death toll was never reached," Sarita said.

"It wasn't much different, in terms of ideology then either. At the time, Japan was on one side of a bunch of allied countries, while America was on another. One didn't want to be conquered, so they dropped a bomb there as well as in Nagasaki, to force the Japanese to submit," Fiona replied. "War doesn't really change, just the times and the people fighting."

"Well said. Why don't we focus on reaching the temple and maintaining a peaceful mindset getting there? Let us honor the fallen in a centered state of mind," Sarita said, changing the subject to brighten up Fiona's sinking mood. The words seemed to have had great effect as Fiona replied, "You're right. We're here to observe and be peaceful. No need for war talks." Sarita observed that while Fiona knew much about war, she absolutely detested it.

A pathway led through some trees and revealed an open field, smooth and well kept, along with the massive white head of Kannon looking at the two. Fiona gasped in awe, completely enamored with such a construct. "We're here at last," she said breathlessly, her eyes wide and focused on the statue. Sarita took a moment to look upon the construct of Kannon and added, "It's truly something else. I never even left my village in my former life. Now here we are across the world, in a different land, in front of something so majestic." Fiona slowly approached the head, as she took in the gentle features of Kannon looking down on her with a peaceful face. As she approached the massive statue, a sensation of chills ran through her, and she felt as though she was being watched. "Sarita, what is happening? Did you feel that?" Fiona asked, unnerved.

"No need to worry. It is the spirits of the area roaming around. None are hostile or wish us any harm," Sarita replied. Fiona felt the presences of many of the spirits all passing by her at once, but calmed down at Sarita's words. "Oh…that's good. Well then, shall we go pay respects inside?" Fiona said. Sarita nodded in response, and the two followed the brick-laden path to the side of the statue where a small set of stairs were. Climbing up them, the two made their way through the door and inside the area. Inside, they found three little rooms. One had miniature statues and candles to the right, a place to sit and or kneel at the visitor's choice in the middle, and a collection of various items and décor to the left. Fiona made her way to the candles and mini statues on the right and pulled out a small one she brought from her hotel. Lighting it up with a match, she put it next to one of the statues in the many rows and bowed her head in a prayer of offering and thanks. As she did, a rush of wind suddenly blew through the inner temple and extinguished all the candlelight. Fiona immediately perked her head up, feeling the strong wind and nervously asked, "What was that?" Sarita calmly but tensely responded, "I'm not sure, but there is a powerful spirit here."

"I can't see it, where is it?" Fiona asked.

"I'll show you through my eyes." Sarita responded, as she merged back into Fiona. Fiona began to feel a strange sensation as her eyesight adjusted to the new darkness. Not only did it adjust, but she could feel and see the blue outline of something standing on the other side of the temple. Startled, Fiona stepped back at the apparition, uneasy and scared at the sight of it. She could make out the features of a man in a hakama outfit that flowed neatly and with great poise. He had a top knot tied up to collect his long hair. Fiona knew enough about Japanese culture to recognize the spirit as either a samurai, or practitioner of bushido.

"It seems we're in the presence of a warrior," Sarita added, as though she'd read Fiona's thoughts.

"A samurai, most likely. Warrior class of Japan centuries ago," Fiona replied.

"What does he want? Can you speak to him?" Sarita appeared in front of Fiona and floated over to the visitor in front of them. She began speaking in a murmured whisper of sorts, one that echoed ethereally in an unknown language Fiona had never heard. The spirit replied in an eerily deeper voice that sounded like it was muddled through water, also in an undiscernible language. The two exchanged words for a time then took a moment of pause. Fiona watched Sarita head back over to her and asked,

"What did he say?"

"He's curious about us. He felt both of our presences and was surprised to see us here at this temple. Also made mention of thinking of you and I as oni, whatever that means." Fiona gulped nervously and replied, "That's not good. He thinks we're demons." Sarita was the one to look off-put then, as she turned to face the spirit of the samurai, who then stood up from his kneeling position. "Sarita, what now?" Fiona asked, her fear starting to rise quickly. "Well, we will see. Spirits can't generally hurt the living if that's what you're worried about. It doesn't mean he still can't affect you, though," Sarita replied. Fiona wasn't sure what was about to happen, but didn't like the way things were going.

Chapter 1

Vacation and Vocation

A good portion of the summer was spent with family amongst the Sigma Pi group, so Sam made it a point to bring the fraternity to the mountain once they had all begun school again. Until that time, they all went their separate ways to go see their families for summer break. Sam himself used some of his time off to practice and train with Hanska, to continuously improve and prepare for a day that Rodrigo would strike again. Things had been relatively peaceful since the incident where he faced off against Bradley. He spent some time with Sara in the area in June, and when July came around, Sam drove with her down to Florida where she could meet his family. Sara came to enjoy the hot weather and constant sunny days that Florida had, as well as being perplexed by the sight of alligators. Mr. and Mrs. Cruz were a very welcoming couple, and happily welcomed Sara and Sam for their visit. Sam lamented his inability to see Luis, his younger brother, with him having departed for basic training in the military, but understood that he had to answer the call. Sara enjoyed the trips to the beaches and getting to eat at the local restaurants in the area, as well as having *horchata* for the very first time.

One evening, Sam and Sara decided to head to the beach to spend the evening together. As the two enjoyed the day out on the sand and water, Sara was absolutely enamored with the scenery. She had never seen such beauty except on TV shows and pictures, let alone her first ever visit to somewhere coastal. Sam on the other hand was rather fond of Fort Lauderdale Beach, for despite being a hotspot for many goers, it was still a lovely place to visit. As the evening came on, Sam and Sara found a nice place on the beach to kick back and relax, watching the sun go down. "Well sweetheart, the night is on its way and young. Anything else you want to do while we're out here?" Sam asked Sara, his arm around her as they sat together looking at the warm, orange sunset sky, sparkling on the ocean.

"We could always peruse the clubs out here. Is Fort Lauderdale as wild as they say?" Sara replied with a sly grin. "Oh yes. The clubs out here get rather crazy. Not to mention, the nightlife booms here while summer is on. Sometimes the people get out of hand, but generally I avoid going to the places `where the craziness like that breaks out. I always ended up going to the restaurants here with Fred, and or the clubs that would let us. They wouldn't serve us, but were okay with us at least being there," Sam replied. Sara excitedly teased, "That's perfect! Sounds like we're going to have a night out on the town then, huh?"

"I suppose so. Now then, should we go change into evening attire before we go?" Sam asked, grabbing their bags. Sara got up and brushed the sand off her legs, as the two headed for their hotel they got for a few days near the beach. The two walked along the sand and enjoyed the orange glow of the sky that turned into a shade of purple as time went on. Walking up the sidewalk on the boardwalk, Sam pulled out the keycard for their room and swiped it in the door marked "103" and opened the door. Once they were both inside, Sam took his clothes out of the bag and laid them on the chair near their bed. The room had a beach color scheme to it, befitting the location where the hotel sat. Eggshell walls held various décor like pictures of the beach, rope net pieces on wooden anchors and canvas paintings of water and sailboats. As Sam went to put his shirt on, he turned around to see Sara looking at him with a sly grin, the top piece of her bathing suit untied on the floor. "Oh! May I help you, madam?" Sam asked, taken by surprise while he stared in admiration of Sara's body. Sauntering over to him, she replied, "I can think of a few ways. Why don't we put getting ready on hold for bit?" A few hours later, Sam was buttoning up his yellow button up shirt with white shorts, while Sara had just gotten out of the shower. There were a few bruises on Sam's collarbone and claw marks on his back, but nothing he minded. Sara had a few marks on her as well, mainly on her chest and shoulders. As she looked in the mirror while drying off, she teased, "Think you did enough of a number on me?" Sara ran her hand over a few of the bite bruises, while Sam tossed her an ointment. "You're a tough girl, right? Use that if it's so bad," Sam teased back. Sara giggled and lightly popped him in the shoulder, saying, You're an ass. I love it, though. You used to be so shy and nervous when I met you." "I don't know. After everything that happened back in Colorado before the end of semester, it was like I had to step up," Sam explained, getting lost in the memories.

"There was a threat present for all of us, and given the essence that came over me, it was either kill or be killed. There was no way I was going to let Rodrigo or Bradley do anything to hurt you guys. Especially you." Sara dried her long red hair with the towel and then leaned onto Sam. "I know. I'm glad that's over." Sam looked down at her and replied, "I hope so as well. He's still out there somewhere, but if he's not here, then I think we're safe."

"Enough talk about that. Why don't we look forward to hitting the clubs tonight? We're going to have an excellent time," Sara stated as she put on her undergarments and slid into an evening dress. The dress had a slit in the side and started below the knees, all the way up to the top. The fabric was soft and flowy, adding to the allure of the light blue color. "You're right. Let's go enjoy a night on the town."

Various colors from the sign lights gave flare and pizzazz to the night, as the two made their way down a line of bars and clubs. The salty air from the ocean carried over to the streets, as people talked and passed by, thus adding to the flow of the nightlife. Sam and Sara made their way down the sidewalk hand in hand, watching the people and cars all pass by as Sara gleefully took in the sights. "Sam," she gasped," I've only seen this stuff in the movies and TV. This is truly something else."

"Yep! This is tropical Florida at some of its finest," Sam replied as the two turned into a bar with a back-deck patio and people Dancing at it. Walking through the doorway, Sam and Sara were soon stopped by the bouncer in black clothes at the door. Both flashed their respective IDs and the burly man let them through. Inside, the scent of various drinks, perfumes and colognes and cool air from the ventilation, pumped through the club. The sound of the bass melded with lights to create an atmosphere of surreal neon energy, inciting the people inside to catch on to the rhythm and Dance with one another. Sara's heartbeat picked up the pace as Sam led her through the club and down a hall, to where a glass double door was. Stepping through, the rush of the warm air from outside hit the two, as the sound faded down to dull thumping from behind the closing glass doors. Sam turned back to Sara, swept his arm before the back-deck with tiki torches and cabana awning, and said, "Welcome to Tapatio's back porch!"

"Sam…this looks so cool!" Sara happily replied, clapping her hands together with her eyes going wide. The scenery was foreign to her, something completely new and she was in love with it. The cabana awnings where made of a tacky make of wood and straw, strewn with white icicle lights around the entire perimeter of the outdoors area. There was an upstairs where a tiki bar was serving cocktails. It had a lounge area for all the club goers with bamboo wicker furniture and wooden barstools. In the center, was a sand pit where people could Dance. Sequestered off to the side, a table was set up with two large pitchers full of beer on each side. At each end, was a person facing off against another in bouncing quarters off the table into the pitchers.

"Well Sara, what do you think?" Sam asked.

"There's nothing like this back home! Oh my God, this is incredible! Come on, let's see if we can get drinks!" Sara eagerly replied before she pulled Sam to the wooden stairs leading to the tiki bar. Upon arrival at the top, the couple approached the bartender and Sam said, "Hey there! Can we get two dark and stormy cocktails, please?"

"Coming right up!" the bartender happily replied as she began pouring the rum and ginger beer with dexterous speed and expertise, before snuggly putting a lime on each copper mug and handing it to the two. Sam slid the bartender a ten-dollar bill, nodded his thanks and lifted his mug to Sara. "Here's to our summer vacation and us, out here enjoying ourselves before we have to go back to Colorado, as well as getting past all of the things that happened during the school year," Sam toasted. Sara met his mug with her own and the two took a sip of their drinks. Sara tasted a rush of sweet, tart, and citrusy fluid all hit her tongue at once. "Sam, I've never had these before, but this could easily be a favorite of mine." "They're excellent to have after a day at the beach. Sits well on the tongue," Sam replied. The two took a seat on the bamboo chairs and looked out on the area in the sand where everyone was Dancing, taking in the sights. "Sam," Sara said after quaffing on her drink. "Are you still going to keep on pursuing computer science when we get back?"

"What brought that on?" Sam replied, surprised by the question. "Sorry. I was just thinking of when we get back. I know you've been frustrated with the classes. I was thinking maybe to go into

another field you'd like?" Sam stretched his legs out a bit and
responded, "I've thought about it. I may switch to something like
archaeology if I get fed up with the tech field. I absolutely love
computers. But the classes aren't enjoyable to learn on it. I've
always had a fascination with history, however."
"Exactly. I mean, you already have the hideout on Mount Elbert, I
bet that'd be an incredible archaeology discovery for the field, if
you so desired to bring it to light."
"There is that, yes. And learning the history on such a thing as the
Jan Damis was quite the story there. Imagine all of the other things
we could find…" Sara watched Sam trail off at his words as he
began to stare into the distance. "Sam, are you going to finish?"
"Yes!" Sam replied, snapping out of his thoughts. "You just gave
me a revelation. Why not switch to archaeology and go find these
things? I'm sure I could get away with doing that as an
archaeology student versus a computer desk lackey."
"Well only if you want to."
"No…it actually makes perfect sense. A lot of sense." Sam took a
swig of his drink and continued, "That's it, I'm switching majors
when I get back. I want to be in the world, not behind a desk."
Sara chuckled and replied, "I'm glad I could help." "I suppose
even you have some bright ideas," Sam teased her. Sara's jaw
dropped and she swatted him with a smile on her face. "You ass!"
"You know I have to mess with you now and then. It'd be boring
if I didn't." Sara grinned and sipped her drink, then replied, "Ugh,
yeah you're right about that. Healthy diss to bliss ratio, right? You
used to not be like this."
"You helped me get there" Sara flung her hair in Sam's face and
she smugly replied, "Well, you are right about that too. I have
appearances to keep up though." "How about we go for a Dance
and enjoy more of the night, as well as celebrate my new career
choice?" Sam said. The two downed their drinks as Sara grabbed
Sam's hand and she replied, "By all means, let's."

On the sand, the two were moving in step and time to the song
playing over the speakers. The pace began to slow as a gentle
acoustic started playing, one which Sam and Sara knew
immediately upon hearing the opening notes. "I love this song,"
Sara said, and she leaned her head onto Sam's shoulder. "Extreme

really dropped a classic with this one," Sam replied, swaying gently with her. Part of the two bonding over the months was the area of music they grew up listening to and liked, which fell into the rock and glam metal scene that was so prevalent over the last ten years. As the two moved, Sam accidently bumped into someone that began shouting at someone else behind him. As Sam turned around to apologize, he saw a man with a short crew cut with a girl next to him, crying. Getting the sense that there was something already wrong, he calmly said to the man, "Sorry for bumping into you, man. That was my fault." The man's eyes were ablaze with anger, his expression contorting as he replied, "First I can't settle things with my girl in peace, now I get some jackass wanting to make me spill my drink?" The guy had a wet splash of beer on his chest, staining his white polo shirt. "I apologize. I didn't mean to bump into you or interrupt your girl. Though, she doesn't seem like it was a pleasant conversation." Sam said.

"It isn't any more pleasant now either, smartass," the man huffed as he turned fully to face Sam. Sam gently motioned for Sara to get back as he tried to further diffuse the situation. By the way, the people were starting to look their way and encroach around the area, Sam didn't think he may have had the option to talk the guy down.

"Burt, for the love of God, don't start another fight tonight!" the woman cried, pleading with him.

"Shut up! Perfect night for a fight!" Burt replied, and Sam could easily sense that he wasn't going to relent. He began to deepen his breathing to not only steady himself for an inevitable fight like Hanska taught him to, but also calm his mind down and get his body ready.

"Dude, I don't want to duke it out. It was my mistake; I'll buy you a drink, we enjoy our night, no one makes a scene," Sam said, now standing his ground and slowly asserting himself while trying to diffuse the situation."

"Shut the hell up, dickhead," Burt replied and made his move. Sam watched Burt's right arm swing wide from the side and immediately ducked under it, his reflexes far faster than he let on." Sam's senses dug into the state of hyperawareness which the ability of the essence lent him, as he could see Burt's attacks at a lowered speed. Sam slipped and dodged several wide swings, all whiffing air, and then countered with a quick left followed by a swift right hook. Burt took the blows on the jaw and staggered, reeling from the speed of such blows. His nose began to leak blood and the people all gathered in closer, now eagerly watching the fight. Burt came in for another try and began throwing more haymakers. Sam weaved and blocked every one of them that came his way and drove another hard right into Burt's face, sending him down on his rear and into the sand.

"Burt, knock it off. It's over," Sam replied, his voice no longer calm.

"You son of a bitch!" Burt spat back, wiping the blood away and getting back up to try yet again. Sam let him swing until Burt was tired and huffing heavily. Sam then drove three body shots into his liver and Burt's face contorted in agony as he dropped again, this time to his knees, doubled over in pain.

"Burt, enough!" the woman cried out as she knelt beside him. "I didn't want to break up with you, idiot! I was simply trying to tell you that I hate when you get drunk like this! You always make a damn scene and then embarrass me. And look what happened now!" Burt coughed and struggled to gain his bearings, as he looked to the woman with a dazed look and replied, "You weren't?"

"No! But you don't hear reason when you're drunk! Maybe I should leave you, though. I've had enough of this crap."

"Please don't babe…I'm sorry," Burt replied as he struggled to get up. A hand extended down to him as Burt looked up. The hand belonged to Sam.

"Let's put this behind us, my man." Sam said gently. Burt nodded, the aggression finally out of his eyes as he took Sam's hand and stood up. Something in the way that Sam spoke to him made Burt humble himself as he said, "I'm sorry, fella. I should not have been like that. I need to go talk with my gal. I got too drunk and acted a fool. You're really polite for someone who can kick ass." Sam smiled and replied, "No hard feelings, my man. Go make things right." Burt staggered off with his lady as Sam turned to see Sara looking at him. Walking up to her, he said, "I'm sorry that happened."

"I'm not. Jeez, just when I think you can't be any more attractive, you do it for me," Sara salaciously replied. "Why don't we head back to our room? Watching you be a savage and a gentleman has me feeling a certain type of way, and you need to do something about it." Sam, not one to catch on to subtle remarks quickly, asked, "What do you mean?" Sara sauntered up to him, grazed her nails on his chest and replied, "What do you think I mean? You're slow on the uptake sometimes."

"Oh! Well, let's not keep you waiting then," Sam replied, "Let's go enjoy the rest of our night alone then, love."

CHAPTER 2

THE IDEOLOGY OF ILLUSIONS

Fiona and Sarita were in a darkened room, the lights having faded out of visibility. Through the thick black miasma, the glowing blue outline of a samurai in armor appeared before the two. A sweeping silence was prevalent around the room, except for the occasional jingling of charms and echoes of voices around the three. The samurai stepped forward to the pair as Fiona and Sarita looked back at the entity.

"You've returned to the shrine. What brings you here yet again?" the samurai asked, his voice deep and resonating within the room. "You fear the precipice of the border between the living world and the dead, and yet you've returned after your last encounter here." Fiona shuddered at the thought of last time they met. Sarita assured her that she could not be hurt by a spirit, but the power his spirit and will carried was no less horrifying. In the previous encounter, the samurai drew a blade of the ethereal kind and attacked. While he did no physical damage, Fiona still felt as through the blade was cutting through her solidly. Sarita had tried to get her to focus on using her own spirit to guard herself, but Fiona was completely overwhelmed. Sarita ended up having to take over Fiona's body to help ward off and escape the samurai. Once Fiona came to in her own body again in her own room, Sarita had explained how the machinations of spirits worked. Despite ghosts being able to do no physical harm, they could still very well attack the mind and spirit. Because Fiona had limited experience with dealing with them, all she could relate to was her own paranormal affinity that she'd had since she was a child. Sarita went over basic meditation practices and explained that one must be very attuned to the spirit plane to be able to deal with ones such as the samurai. While most didn't have the capability to be strong, there were exceptions where certain ghosts holding on to strong emotions from the past life were involved, and they were to be reckoned with. The will of the spirit was universal for the living and dead, and the more force of will one had, the stronger the spirit was inevitably. Sarita, being the druid medium of her old tribe, wanted to meet other spirits to possibly get answers on finding an old essence. To this end, Sarita wished to make Fiona more durable and capable of handling not only essences, but spirits. Fiona was taught on how to make her own spirit more sound against others, and that visualizing it while maintaining a strong calm, was a good technique in dealing with others. Sarita also figured it would be a good test to make Fiona grow in her own abilities beyond the essence realm. A few days of practice, in between Fiona meeting with the contacts she needed to for Mr. Viejas, proved rather effective. While Fiona struggled a bit with her essence manipulation, she was a naturally gifted spiritualist. The concept of strengthening spirit and becoming more attuned and aware came to her like a fish learning to swim. Once Sarita felt Fiona was capable enough of dealing with the spirit, she suggested they return to the temple and confront him. Fiona, full of fear of how the last time went, agreed but had great unease about doing so, especially at night. Sarita could only encourage her to use what she had learned. Two days later, they ended up back at the temple. Fiona appeared calm as the samurai appeared again, and seemingly sucked all the candlelight out of the temple. "Great warrior, we're not here to quarrel. I have questions for you," Sarita asked.

"Questions? You trespass upon this temple that I was charged to look after, with your presence here, yet again? Most unwelcome," the samurai replied. Fiona, terror forming in the pit of her stomach, steeled her nerves and began breathing to calm down. She knew he was not capable of physically hurting her, which gave her more capacity to focus on her spirit's calmness. The samurai drew his blade again and readied himself in a middle-level posture, ready to advance and strike. Fiona, having no weapons on her, grabbed a wooden stick from one of the corners and readied herself. Focusing hard on visualizing her own spirit coming out to battle alongside her, a faint red glow surrounded her body, giving off an eerie scintilla of red wisps. Yet, she felt alert and alive. The samurai charged forth and brought his blade down, only to be stopped by Fiona's wooden pole. The very feat surprised her, amazed the sword didn't cut through. "That's it, Fiona! You spirit is at the forefront! Do not lose focus and hold your ground!" Sarita cried out proudly. Fiona felt her confidence skyrocket from such an act. She had managed to block the samurai's sword with her own spirit! Coupled with having experienced the samurai before, Fiona felt much less worried and began to refocus on her maintaining her calm. The samurai came again at her with a deliberate overhead blow, and Fiona stepped to the side, wildly swinging back. She'd had little battle experience in her life, but wasn't afraid to stand toe to toe with the samurai. The warrior came on again with another series of blows, many of which Fiona scrambled to deflect or dodge. She swore that the strikes would come upon her quicker with each hit, but her senses started to heighten, and blocking became easier. The samurai paused, seemingly analyzing her newfound prowess. "I'm not afraid of you anymore! We're not going to leave until you answer Sarita's questions!" Fiona cried out. The red glow around her body began to brighten as the samurai took pause from any movement. A long moment of silence passed before the samurai said, "You have courage…this is admirable. How do I know that you're not here as an evil spirit, though?"

"I'm not an evil spirit. I have a spirit with me here, yes, not unlike you. But I am not here to cause any harm," Fiona replied, her gaze remaining unbroken towards the samurai's facepiece. "I see. Then what is your purpose here?"

"I know I'm a gaijin that brought a spirit here, but I have no intent on damaging this temple. I only came to pay respects. Tell me, why are you still in the world of living?"

"I died long ago defending the temple from robbers that wanted to come and loot it. They were from a rival clan that wanted some sort of item that came from the west here." Fiona's face twisted with confusion as she replied, "An item from the west? Why would a temple like this have something from the west?"

"I'm not sure. Long ago, it was rumored that there was some sort of clan within the country, that had an ability to turn into giant cats of some sort. How they ever got the power is beyond me, if such a thing is real. One of our own countrymen, actually. Within this temple, they hid some sort of relic from the west. Looters came for it one day, and I didn't want the temple desecrated by their filthy hands." Sarita walked forward and asked, "Great warrior, we are not here to violate this sacred place of worship. I am Sarita of the Parduska Clan, from a place out west, possibly the same as which you speak. Please, do not attack anymore. Let us have conversation on the matter." The samurai lowered his guard a bit but did not withdraw his blade. "You know of these shape shifters?"

"I do. I hail from their clan. My friend here is not only a bearer of their essence on my behalf, but is learning more about it as well. We are traveling across the world to get answers. Behold." Sarita immediately changed form into that of a sleek leopard, which put the samurai back on edge. "You are one of them? Are you a yōkai?" the wary warrior asked.

"No, I'm not an evil spirit. I simply have the ability to shapeshift with my friend here," Fiona replied. "Like I said, I have nothing but reverence for your culture and ways. I am simply here to pray and pay respects, my friend is here to get answers." The samurai lowered his guard and replied, "I can sense your intentions, and they are indeed not malevolent. You are a strange woman, but not evil. Very well. Do you seek this relic that has been here for centuries?"

"I didn't even know such a thing was here until you told us to be honest, but it may help my friend of the spirits, here," Fiona replied. Sarita shifted back into human form and asked, "Great warrior, what is your name?"

"Gotaro. Gotaro of the Mountain. It has been some time since a foreign spirit has been within this sacred temple of Kannon-kami."

"I am Sarita of the Parduska Clan, and this is Fiona Marois. I come from Peru and she hails from America. We do not wish to seem like we are trespassing. Would you be willing to show us where the relic lies?" Gotaro withdrew his blade and replied, "What are your intentions with it?"

"Considering it may very well be from my lands, take it back with me and study it to better understand my history," Sarita replied. "Surely as one so bound to the code of honor and legacy, you understand wanting to reclaim an item of great importance to you."

"I do," Gotaro agreed, Sarita's appeal to his honor having worked. "Come with me, I will show you." The darkness around the room faded away in the blink of an eye, as the candlelight and outlines of shapes returned to normal. Gotaro walked over to a podium where a table was and pointed down at it. "Under this table is a hatch that goes lower into the temple. It's been hidden from the public view here but some of the monks still go to visit on occasion. Enter here and I will guide you." Fiona walked over to the wooden table and moved back a few feet. Sure enough, there was an old wooden door with iron braces and a ring handle. Fiona grabbed the cold metal ring and pulled with great effort, managing to open the hatch. A cool gust of wind rose from the dark void, as Fiona took one of the candles on the nearby shelves and held it into the space. The glow of candlelight revealed a dark stone passage that was easily accessible. Fiona sat down and lowered herself in, the height distance only a matter of five feet or so. Once her feet hit the stone, Gotaro appeared in front of her and started leading the women down the stone passage. "This is an old passage that was used during the wars in the Edo era. The monks would hide down here and protect villagers and possessions while the samurai fought. I was one of the ones tasked with guarding the temple. To this day, I still do." The stonework was smooth and well cut out as the trio continued on. After a minute, they arrived at an open chamber. There were benches and seats, as well as various items around the area. Sarita's eyes immediately locked onto one made of metal, with the familiar writing of her tribe. It was a copper bar, that showed the etching of a leopard, as well as writing in her tribe's language. "This is it. No doubt, the spirit stone of my clan," Sarita breathlessly whispered. Fiona moved up next to Sarita and inspected it before asking, "What does it do?"

"It's a copper bar that was used to focus on spirit meditation, as well as for warding off evil spirits and communicating with other essence users across great distances. No doubt a particularly important relic of the Parduska Clan."

"I see. Gotaro, may we take this relic of Sarita's with us? We have no want of anything else, nor disturbing your temple," Fiona asked Gotaro. "If this is indeed the item you look for from your clan, then you may. I will not stop this returning to the rightful owner." Fiona held the copper bar as Sarita touched it and said a few words in her tribe's language. The bar began to glow green as the etchings and writing lit up. The copper bar was no bigger than a bar of soap, as Fiona held the glowing relic. She felt her connection with the spirit plane grow even deeper simply by holding it. "You speak the truth…that is indeed your item. I have only seen it do this one other time…and that was when the previous owner that brought it here hid it. No doubt, you are the rightful owners," Gotaro said. He then lowered himself to the ground and prostrated himself before the two. "Forgive me for my earlier hostility. I wasn't sure what your intentions were before, but you have proven yourself truly honorable. Please accept my humblest apologies."

"Rise, Gotaro. There is no need for that. You were simply protecting the temple," Sarita said in a voice that carried an undercurrent of regality in it. Gotaro rose and replied, "Why don't we go back to the main area of the temple and talk more? I would like to get to know both of you better. It isn't often I get to commune with the living and a fellow spirit in such direct fashion. Most don't even know I'm around."

"That sounds incredible! I have so many questions about the temple and the history here!" Fiona excitedly replied.

"I'd like to know more about the essence user that was here as well. My tribe started small but eventually spread among the world. Please, let us discuss more." Sarita said.

CHAPTER 3

BACK TO SCHOOL

By fall, everyone that went to Keystone University had returned for the semester and classes began again. The members of Sigma Pi had reunited, and shared how their summer vacations went with one another. Fred had gone to Puerto Rico with Hailey for a week, and then went to individually visit their respective families. Fred, having been home around the same time that Sam was with Sara, ended up meeting with them before they headed back to Colorado. Steve McOrwell, the short blond-haired member with a stocky build, green eyes, and rugged build, had gone back home to Minnesota for the summer, to go fishing and camping with his dad. Donte Michaels, the president of Sigma Pi, spent his summer up in New York with his cousins, and was excited to have returned to Colorado. The days passed from early September to later in October, the initial blur of reacclimating to school life passing the time. Sam had switched his major from computers to archaeology, and was much more in his element. The history classes came naturally to him.

One evening, the Sigma Pi all gathered in the main area of the fraternity house due to Sam wanting to call a meeting with them. As they all gathered around, Sam waited until they were all present and comfortable. Once everyone was accounted for, Sam began what he wanted to say. "Good evening, guys. I wanted to have you gather up to talk about Mount Elbert, and the things that happened earlier in the year. I've done research on that place, and I think we need to keep an eye on it from time to time."

"That was the place where that Rodrigo guy and Bradley hid out, right? Where we made the hike to get to?" Donte asked.

"Yes. I don't think Rodrigo will be back anytime soon there, considering he knows we know. However, he is still at large and that worries me some. I'm not trying to drag anyone into something they don't want to get involved in, I'm just trying to make you all aware that he's still a threat."

"Sam, we whipped his ass before, we can sure as hell do it again," Donte said, taking a swig of his beer and prompting a round of laughter from the Sigma Pi. Sam chuckled himself and replied,

"We did, yes. I'm not saying we're incapable, far from it. I just want to research more into the history of the shifters, and the abilities that come with."

Donte nodded, then spoke, "I get where you're coming from. We appreciate the concern, and we're here to let you know you we got your back. Steve can just hunt the bastard if he comes prowling around here. While I was in New York, I visited the gym my cousin trains at, and got back into pad and bag work. We can always put on the gear and go a few rounds if you feel like we need to train you up." Sam beamed and excitedly replied, "I'd love that! You got back into boxing over the summer?"

"Yeah man. That encounter with Rodrigo made me realize I was almost out of my league. I don't ever want to go down fighting if my life depends on it. Not only for myself, but for you and the rest of the fellas. We're all here together, that's what brothers do. We look out for one another."

"Well, I'll definitely drink to that," Sam agreed as the guys all shouted their cheers and took a swig. Downing a quaff, Sam added, "I'm grateful for you guys. Truly. There's nothing better than having a brotherhood to fall back on when things get rough."

"Sam, I know we've only known the fellas a year compared to how far back we go, but I feel they're as close to us as we're close ourselves," Fred added, clapping a hand on his shoulder. "I guess that settles that, then," Sam concurred with a smile. "Well, I plan on hitting Mount Elbert this weekend; if anyone is free and wants to join, I want to look more into the hideout there. Anything to better understand the history and prepare for things. Rodrigo won't be gone forever. Especially if I have the seal."

"I'll roll with you, Sam," Fred said. "Let's roll in the morning on Saturday, and then be back around later afternoon. Sigma Pi is having the autumn cookout, and there's no way in hell we're missing that."

****

Somewhere in the mountains of Washington, a man in a suit and bowler hat walked into a log mountain house that sat in a hidden away spot in the mountains. The sky was gray and foggy, with a cold chill to it due to the location and fresh rain that had fallen. There were tall trees that surrounded the house, affording it extra cover on the mountain. "Rodrigo, tell me why you always seek to have places that are so isolated from the public. I get it, we can shift into giant cats, but does that really warrant being out in the middle of nowhere?" the man asked, stepping away from the entryway and onto the stone floor that was neatly crafted. Rodrigo, dressed in a long sleeve black shirt and gray cargo pants, was smoking out of a pipe, and having a glass of wine as he looked up from his book and saw the man walk across the living room. "Mr. Viejas, I see you've returned from your blackjack excursion," he said, running a hand through his black hair that was neatly cut and trimmed since going into business with his fellow shifter. "I like it out here. Remember, I come from a tribe that lived in the wild. Nature has a special place in my heart. And come on, this is a wonderful house."

"Well, I can't argue that. I much prefer my place out in the city," Mr. Viejas agreed as he went to grab himself a glass from the large kitchen. A decanter of whiskey was on the smooth granite countertop, and he pulled the top off to pour himself a bit. Taking a sniff, Mr. Viejas then said, "This smells like an older batch. I see your taste for fine things has finally started to translate into the times well enough." Rodrigo nodded, took another puff of his pipe, and replied, "I have you to thank for helping me modernize and adapt, as well as to going into business with you."

"Ah, I should be thanking you! Becoming a shifter has greatly helped me, considering I can now sense players on the table and their tells much easier, as well as having access to shifting into a leopard. Plus, going back to the ruins of your old tribe to collect your stores of gold and treasures, was the main boost to getting this partnership off the ground."

"Hence why we have a partnership, my friend. We greatly amplified one another, and currently have someone out in Japan laying even more groundwork for us."

Rodrigo smiled and replied. "Ah yes, Fiona. How is she doing?" Mr. Viejas sipped from his whiskey glass and responded, "She's doing quite well! Miss Marois and I spoke earlier, and she actually found a relic of your tribe." Rodrigo's eyes lit up as he asked, "What did she find?"

"The spirit stone, which I'm a little confused as to why it's a stone when it's made of copper?"

"The spirit stone, the druid medium's old artifact. Is metal not of the earth to be a stone?"

"Eh…not entirely wrong, but I'm not here to argue syntax. Anyways, what does it do?"

"The spirit stone was a blessed relic from my tribe that let essence users talk over distances. The druid medium of the tribe was able to channel such energy and perform the act." Mr. Viejas raised an eyebrow and asked, "Do you think Fiona has the essence of the druid medium, then?"

"I would bet on it. I won't know for sure until she returns, considering you've done most of the interaction with her since we've begun this business. The war chief has already been sealed away and Sam has the iron spiritualist. That leaves the stoic sage out there. Once we find them, all five essence users will be with us again."

"It's safe to say she probably is. Fiona has had more interactions with the spirits of the land where she's at. Fiona even managed to take on the spirit of a samurai and then talk with him. I must say, rather impressive!"

"That's great to know. Fiona has proven a wonderful asset to us." Rodrigo marked the page he was reading, and closed the book in his lap. Turning to face out the window, he sighed at the sights and said, "This is quite different from the jungles and temples from my homeland, but I enjoy it."

"Rightfully so, Rodrigo. What's the next part of your plan?" Viejas inquired.

"I plan to find the final essence user and bring him to our cause, then pay Sam another visit and ask if he'd like to join us once more. Should he not, well then we'll get the essence from him and move forward to begin our society once more."

"Oh? I didn't think you wanted to split the essences up this time around?"

"I don't. I will hunt down my old texts and relearn the ritual that initially brought the powers about in this world."

Mr. Viejas took a sip of his drink and cast Rodrigo a curious glance. "The ritual that requires human sacrifice?" he asked pensively.

"It is. Now, I understand it is a thing that isn't gone about lightly, and there are implications for murdering people. This is what I propose to you, my friend. We gather inmates slated for execution across the country, find a way to buy them off their sentence, and use them for sacrifices." Mr. Viejas smiled and replied, "Ethical, at the very least. Keeps you out of hot water, as well. Now that's a plan I can get behind." Rodrigo grinned back and said, "I realize that people don't worship or know of my tribe's old belief systems, and that something like that doesn't sit well with society. Society is much more…polite. Civilized. I come from a tribe where war and death were common."

"Society is certainly not how things were for you all those years ago. But that kind of plan can work. I can start making calls to at least get our feet in the doors of prisons that aren't against letting us take their inmates off their hands."

"I would greatly appreciate that. Once Fiona returns from Japan, let her go on vacation for a time. I know she's not privy to the inner machinations of how I do things, and it's probably better that way. You keep interacting with her, not letting her know too much beyond the front of traveling business. She isn't ready to face the reality of things yet." Mr. Viejas nodded and replied, "If that is what you wish, it shall be done. Miss Marois will continue to establish leads for us to set up future bases of operations, for the new society we will create. Speaking of, have you a plan for gathering more to your cause?" Rodrigo took a drag from his pipe and replied, "Of course. I've begun offering intern positions for our company out in Seattle, for people to work with us. They'll be relations members; kind of what Fiona does. We'll have them go out and offer membership to prospects, and feel out who would like a way to gain new insight and power over their lives. Like how preachers and those motivational speakers you all have nowadays do. Except we can actually change lives with the essences."

"The lead by charisma play; that's a wise move to make in swaying those to your side. No doubt, I'd imagine you'd give them glimpses of the abilities they stand to gain, once you sway them so?" Mr. Viejas asked, his intrigue further deepening.

"Yes. People are very skeptical unless presented with facts. I'm sure that showing them some of the capabilities of the essences would do great things in bringing others onboard. No way to refute a man that can shift into a large cat, no? Couple that with selling them on how they can achieve it too to make their lives better, and we've got the beginnings to a new secret society to form."

"Rodrigo, I'm most impressed with that. That is certainly an excellent way to bring on new numbers. From what it sounds like, you've already got some starting up, yes?"

"I do. College graduates are quite easy to sway. A bit of incentive with promises of a dream job and structure to their lives, and they want to devour it up like a fresh meal. Of course, this is all thanks to you helping me get used to the modern world. I'd still be trotting out in my old robes if it weren't for you."

"I couldn't leave a man such as you to go about in this world without knowing how it works. You need to have a position of importance, and that means looking the part to the modern world."

****

Sam and Fred arrived at Mount Elbert, and headed to one of the passages within the mountain that gave them a shortcut to the top, where the main hideout was. The stone passages all had the writing which Sam was familiar with, from the last time he was there. Fred was in awe, not believing what he was seeing.

"You weren't kidding, man. This is wild," Fred said, as the two continued through the stone passages with their flashlights. "Wait until we get to the main place where the remains of the wyvern are," Sam replied, eliciting further surprise for Fred.

"A wyvern? Like a damn dragon?"

"The very one."

Fred shivered at the idea of dragons living and realized that it wasn't a far-off fantasy if they did. After all, if Sam could turn into a leopard, there wasn't much he was willing to discredit anymore. After an hour or so, the two made their way into an open area, which Sam immediately recognized as the hideout. Before the two, the skeleton of a massive wyvern lay down on its side, one of the wings protruding upwards and through the ceiling.

"That's the location just under the top of the mountain, where we camped last year before things went nuts," Sam said. "You weren't kidding, Sam. This is incredible," Fred replied as he went to inspect the skeleton. Sam felt a shift in the air as he looked around, sensing that something living was nearby. "Fred…I got the feeling we may not be alone here," Sam replied as he began to calm himself with focused breathing.

"What do you mean?" Fred replied, unsure of what Sam was getting at. Hanska appeared before Sam and said, "There is a powerful presence around. Be careful. It's full of life force and in great quantities." Sam walked around slowly, feeling the air with his senses, a trick gotten from training with Hanska. As he did, a dull rumble shook the top of the mountain, causing a few pebbles to fall from the ceiling. "What the hell was that?" Fred replied, rolling up his sleeves to prepare for a potential fight. "I'm not sure, but that wasn't anything ordinary," Sam said. Shifting into his leopard form, he raced for the stairs leading to the alcove where one could get a better look, and access to the top of the mountain. Within moments, Sam had arrived at the stone balcony area and slowly crept up the path that led to the mountaintop. Despite the sun being out, a brisk chill was present in the autumn air, further affected by the altitude. What Sam saw while peeking out, set his nerves on edge. A wave of awe and terror washed through him. There was a large winged reptilian beast, with purple colored skin that shone brilliantly in the sun. Powerful legs corded in muscle, rippled and flexed with each movement, as piercing yellow eyes stayed fixated on something in the ground. Its massive wings were tucked in, along with its tail, showing a relaxed posture. "Hanska, am I looking at what I think I am?" Sam asked in his mind. "You are. A living wyvern. And here I thought they all faded into extinction. If I were you, it would be wise to switch back into your human form. They hate the shifters with a passion." Sam did just that, reverting to his human form and could feel the immense life presence of the majestic creature before him. Yet, despite his fear, Sam knew the wyvern could have answers.

"Oh, good morning there!" Sam said after taking a breath and stepping atop the mountain in the most causal manner he could muster. In doing so, he startled the wyvern as the great creature snapped its eyes towards him. "Whoa, I'm not here to cause any trouble."

"What are you doing here, human? I didn't see you on the trails when I was flying around," the wyvern replied, his voice deep and gravelly. "Hiking. It's a public trail, as well as a famous one to visit. I didn't know dragons were real though…my question is what are you doing here?" Sam replied, trying to reverse the question on it. "I am visiting my ancestor's grave here. I was told by my clan that there are humans of a certain kind that walk the earth again, and to go seek answers here," the wyvern replied, showing unease at being in the open before a human. "Clan…hold on, you have a clan?" Sam asked, his feigned curiosity becoming more real by the second. "There's more of you? What are you looking for?"

"That's my business. Very incredible feat to not be seen by a wyvern, by the way. Humans aren't exactly the stealthiest of creatures." Sam decided to take a gamble and establish some understanding to diffuse the tension in the air and said, "I read some of the history here. Legend tells of a wyvern that rests here. With you here, that must confirm it, no?"

"Oh ho! And what do you know of history?" the wyvern replied, taking the bait. Sam decided to up the ante and continued with a more serious tone, "Your ancestor's name. Illixus. Am I right?"

The wyvern's eyes grew wider as it replied, "How do you know? History has been kept to only remnants of the old alliance. The Dracosapiens…Are you…one of them?" the wyvern asked, now on the backfoot.

"Technically, no. I'll be honest with you; my girlfriend's family is, though. I learned much of the history from them, as well as experiences from here." The wyvern turned to fully face Sam and approached a few steps before saying, "You're no ordinary human, then. But why would they share that with you?" Sam paused, then decided to go all in with his parlaying. "Because the Oro Luna was up here and activated. Rodrigo lives again."

"He does?! That's impossible!"

"It's not. If anything, he used to be here. I know because I encountered him before."

"You did?"

Sam nodded and replied, "That bastard attacked my friends and tried to have me done in as well."

"I see…you speak the truth then. Tell me, what is your name? Anyone that has this much knowledge of things is at least worth knowing."

"Sam. Sam Cruz. May I ask you yours?"

"Loxa," the wyvern replied. "Tell me Sam, how much do you know of the Jan Damis?"

"As far as I know, they were the society of shifters Rodrigo had that affected world events and had a powerful network. The Dracosapiens were responsible for taking them down."

"You know much. Tell me, what side do you stand on?"

"Loxa, I'll be honest with you. I think he's trying to bring back that society. I want nothing to do with it. I've been cursed with one of the essences because of the Oro Luna."

"You were?" Loxa asked, his eyes widening. Sam held his hands up and replied, "Yes, I have the ability to shift. I didn't ask for it, it happened when I was attacked up here and the seal broke. I'm not with Rodrigo."

"Hm…that does present a strange case. The Dracosapiens were vehemently against the shifters…but these are different times, and you've done nothing to be labeled untrustworthy so far. But how can I trust you're not with Rodrigo?" Sam began to take his jacket off and pulled up his shirt, revealing the claw mark scars on his chest. "The bastard had one of his lackeys come for me and try to kill me for my essence," Sam responded, vitriol in his voice. Loxa looked the young man up and down and replied, "Your intentions feel true. I detect no dishonesty or malicious intent from you."

"I have no reason to lie to you. If anything, I'm allied with the descendants of the Dracosapiens. The DuMont clan; do they ring a bell to you?"

"The name indeed does sound familiar to me. My family has told me of the major people that took place in the rebellion against the Jan Damis, including that clan name." Sam nodded, and thought of his next move to turn the conversation into further exploration into how they could help one another. Then the idea hit him. "You said you seek answers here, right? Perhaps we can help each other. What other answers do you need? I might be able to help you," he said to Loxa. The wyvern had a pensive look on his face for a time before replying, "Well, you seem to have already given me most of them, which I'm grateful for. I came here to see about the seal, since we sensed that the energy of the essence had come back into the world of recent. The fact that the seal has loosed Rodrigo was most of it. Now, it's a matter of finding him."

"Do you think he'll try to bring back the Jan Damis?" Sam asked, already sort of knowing the answer. "Without question. Men that have power will always seek more," Loxa replied, before he went to remove a scale from his long, powerful tail. He tossed it to Sam and the young man caught it in kind. "Hold on to this. I would like to find you again if need be. You could be a useful ally down the line."

"I'd like that.

"Then it seems we're not done with Rodrigo after all, confirming my own suspicions as well." Loxa unfurled his wings and hunched forward as he said, "It was good to meet you, Sam. I will seek you out again in the future; farewell." The mighty wyvern took two equally mighty wingbeats and started to take flight in the air, the wind from the movement rushing powerfully past Sam. Sam had never seen something so beautiful, yet so dangerous in his life until then. A real-life wyvern: they indeed lived! As he watched the great creature gain altitude and fly off into the distance, he sighed in relief, grateful that he had made friends with him instead of the opposite. Fred appeared next to Sam and asked with a pale face, "W-what was that? Did I just see a real-life dragon?"

CHAPTER 4

THE NEXT MOVE

Fiona had flown back from Japan by late fall, having established a place for Mr. Viejas and the company to work overseas. It had been quite a few months since Fiona had returned stateside, but she absolutely loved her time spent in Japan. She had often visited Gotaro at the shrine, having pleasant conversations and learning more about the history of the country, as well as practicing her spirit abilities afforded her by Sarita. Mr. Viejas had met her at the airport in Seattle and given her a warm welcome back, as well as filled her in on all that happened while she was away. Mr. Viejas explained that the base of operations had moved to Washington state, and that they were gaining new interns to work with the company. Fiona expressed great excitement at such a thing, knowing they were expanding as a team and moving forward with the company. Expansion often brought with it great things, and Fiona looked forward to having more cohorts to eventually work with. Mr. Viejas had also given her a large wad of cash once they went out for dinner, which surprised the young woman. "What's this for?" she asked. "I already get my paycheck from the company."

"A bonus for such diligent work," Mr. Viejas replied with a smile on his face. "You've been away for quite some time, and it's going to be Thanksgiving next week. A token of my appreciation for all you've done." Fiona beamed and said, "Thank you, Mr. Viejas. What's the next move?"

"First, you're going to go home and take some time to enjoy the holidays with your family. The holidays are coming along fast, and i don't want you overworked. When Thanksgiving is over, I'll have you go on a more local, shorter assignment in Colorado. Nothing too difficult at all."

"Very well. I can do that no problem. What's the task there?"

"Nothing to worry about at this time. You're home safely; let us focus on you being able to relax and unwind from such an arduous trip. We can worry about the assignment after."

Meanwhile, down in Peru, Rodrigo was walking through a forest of large trees and lush greenery. He knew for certain that the place he was at, was the old location where his tribe once existed. The trees had grown in height since he had been there. The paths he once knew existed, had been lost to time. Much of the area had been nearly impossible to discern for Rodrigo, had he not brought and studied a map to get there. Using his own essence, Rodrigo began to sense and feel out the energy of the place. Without doubt, it felt like the very same energy Rodrigo knew of in a former life. Making his way further through the trees, he spotted something green and mossy up ahead. The moss had settled on what looked like a massive mound, and by the looks of it, Rodrigo could tell that it was indeed an old temple that belonged to his old tribe. Walking through the bushes, Rodrigo approached the great construct, amazed that it had stood the test of time and hadn't collapsed. Sighing in admiration, Rodrigo pulled out a flashlight and walked inside. The light shone on overgrown vegetation and moss that had taken over the stone temple. Rodrigo felt a surge of ancient energy and the presence of his former clansmen all there. Making his way through the main room towards a corridor, the stone passage wreathed in flora led him to a smaller room, with stone braziers and an altar. "At last, the place I seek," Rodrigo said to himself as he walked up to the altar ahead. There, just as he had left it so long ago, was a knife, ornately decorated and meticulously crafted. There were engravings on the curved blade which seemed to glow green when Rodrigo touched it. "This is it. My ceremonial knife for the bestowment of essence powers to others. I can't believe that after centuries, it remains untouched by time. This is good news. Now to return to Washington and begin building the empire we need." Rodrigo slipped the knife into his belt and took another look around the room. He felt the sense of familiarity wash over him, thought back to his tribe, and the Jan Damis. Where the original essence users of his old tribe were once five, there would now be far more without having to split them. Rodrigo began to head out of the temple and headed off to look for other remnants of his tribe. Later that day, Rodrigo caught a plane out of South America and landed in Mexico for a layover. As he did, he sensed another essence in the area. He wasn't sure how far away, but could still feel the pull, the familiar feeling of when one essence was not too far away from another. "Hm...I may need Mr. Viejas to do some detective work for me here.

Another essence here? That may very well be the blood beast, the final missing puzzle piece. If we could get him on our side, then the last thing to do would be to get Sam and have all the essences together again. I will make note of this."

By Thanksgiving week, Fiona had returned home to Vancouver and visited her parents for the holidays. They enjoyed a wonderful dinner together and were happy that Fiona had returned home after such a long journey to Japan. Fiona was particularly delighted she was able to help her parents with the Thanksgiving dinner, grabbing all the food with money earned from her Japan trip. She had regaled her parents with tales of being in the country, how beautiful and peaceful it was there, while leaving out the details on the encounters with spirits there. Once dinner had finished up, Fiona went to her old room that she grew up in before she had moved out. Once up there, Fiona went over to her old desk and sat down to read a manga she got while she was in Japan. The story was about a kid that set foot into a boxing ring, and began his journey to becoming a champion with his friends. As she read, Sarita appeared before her. "Well Fiona, Japan was certainly eye-opening. It was nice to be able to talk to another spirit, considering I haven't seen one in so long," she said rather pleasantly. Fiona looked up from her book and replied, "You were sealed away, right?"

"I was, yes."

"What was it like in the seal? Couldn't you speak to the other essences?"

"No. The seal keeps us each individually contained. Not only that, but our essences were scattered into fragments during the last time the Jan Damis ran wild. When we were all split into fragments, we could not exist wholly. Thus, the memories of the five original essence users were hazy and incomplete. Only I remembered most of what happened, being a separate spirit from my essence."

"I see, that makes sense. Do you know if all of the essences are back into the world?" Fiona asked.

"It's hard to say, but I would bet on it. I can confirm us, as well as Mr. Viejas at the very least."

"Where is the Oro Luna? If the seal that held you all in released you, then where's the seal?"

"I'm not sure. You'd have to ask Mr. Viejas himself. He'd likely know more." Fiona nodded her understanding and then looked out the window. A gentle snow flurry had begun, along with cascaded snowflakes that were lit by streetlights against the night sky. "Tell me, Sarita," Fiona said after a pause of silence, "What was the tribe like? What was your way of life like?" Sarita floated over to Fiona's bed and began, "Well, centuries ago, we were just a tribe. There was nothing too fancy about us. We were a warring group that fended off other invading tribes trying to take our place in the jungle that we had. The location we lived at was ideal cover from invaders and some natural predators. Other than fighting off the other tribes, we lived in peace and prosperity. One day, around the time we changed leaders, and Rodrigo had taken up the role of our tribe chieftain, he discovered the ritual of the leopard."

"Ritual of the leopard?" Fiona asked.

"Yes. It was a ritual that demanded a live sacrifice to create the essences imbued with the power of the leopard. Not only did it bestow the shifting abilities, but it also made our tribe completely unrivalled in doing so. Rodrigo grew power hungry after making the first three and wanted to continue making them."

"And how did he do that?" Fiona asked.

"He started by offering the rival chieftain, the Jaguar King Paolo of the other tribe, a chance to gain his own power, the very first essence. However, instead of creating a new essence from the king's sacrifice, Rodrigo intertwined the very life force from the sacrifice and weaved the essence into himself. He became known as the immortal Leopard King Rodrigo, for age could not affect him afterwards. Only a fatal disease or a mortal wound from another essence user could've stopped him."

"Well, if he used the lives of his enemies, I guess it wasn't so bad. I wouldn't do it, but he was a chieftain of a tribe, not me."

"It wasn't a problem, until he started using our own people."

"He did what?!" Fiona asked, surprised at Sarita's statement. Sarita glanced at her solemnly and replied, "Once the word had spread to other tribes that we had gained the powers of the essences to turn into leopards, we were attacked far less. Peace had come to our village. Without enemies coming along, Rodrigo wanted to continue to bolster the numbers of the essence users. He initially had his war chief, Piero, and the iron spiritualist, Hanska, both having gained essences from two powerful tribe leaders of other groups. Then came the shadow master from a shaman of another warring tribe, who possessed a small degree of clairvoyance. After that, the others stopped trying to invade us, and that's when Rodrigo used our own villagers." "That's horrible. How could he?"

"In his view, to further strengthen our village. It was the sacrifice of Hanska's fiancée and my sister, Marcela, which got to me personally." Sarita somberly said, her voice growing soft and quiet. Fiona could feel the sadness coming from Sarita as she gently replied, "I'm sorry that happened. That's horrible. Was he apprehended?"

"He fled the village when Hanska caught on to the sacrifice and led the others to revolt against Rodrigo. Piero fled with him and together, the two would begin to work on forming the Jan Damis. Rodrigo swore to return for our essences when we were older or deceased, and with his immortality, he did just that. Once he had gathered the essences of the others, he created one more from a wild and savage warrior animal of another tribe he took over, known as the blood beast."

"The blood beast?"

"Yes. He was a nature guardian leopard that when sacrificed, became an essence capable of tracking people by scent, and granted them absurdly high battle prowess."

"I see. And your spirit outlived the others by merging with your essence, right?"

"That is correct."

"How did you do it?"

"The spirit stone. I intertwined and anchored my spirit to the world here with it, using similar writing akin to the ritual of the leopard. By engraving the stone with the writing of the tribe and using some of my own blood, I was able to tie myself to it and stay in the world of the living, beyond being just an essence to be tied to a person. I could roam freely on my own."

"I understand. That's quite a bit of a tale and history, Sarita. I'm sorry you had to experience such things."

"Don't apologize yet, Fiona. If the essences are back in the world, it stands to reason that Rodrigo is too. Which likely means that he'll want to form a new society, after the old one was stopped. Who knows which essence is where now? All I know is if my essence is with you, the others are in other people."

"Do you think we'll find the others?" Fiona asked. "It is highly likely they will show up with time. Given that the Oro Luna has brought the other essences back, I wouldn't rule it out. It ultimately depends on which individuals have what essence. That could determine our future interactions with them. That much I can swear by."

"Can you tell me about each essence? I'd like to know more if they're back in the world." Sarita nodded and responded, "I will. It would behoove you to know as such. There are five main essences as well as that of the leopard king. The iron spiritualist was known for having great physical strength, fighting spirit and awareness of self. The war chief could bolster the spirits of those around him and had great tactical fighting knowledge. The shadow master is one who can create illusions, conceal their presence, and project their shadow as a second set of eyes, almost like a body double. Mr. Viejas is the only other confirmed essence holder I know. The blood beast is a vicious essence that had animal like senses, much more acute than even regular shifters, as well as vicious hunting instinct and durability. Finally, you know some of what the druid medium does, since you have my essence. Astral projection, sensing of and communing with other spirits and limited possession."

"Hold on, I can possess other people?" Fiona asked, bewildered. "Indeed, you can. You have yet to learn how to astral project, which is a needed facet in learning how to take someone over."

"How do I do it? Teach me."

"Well, we would have to start with getting your projection down. However, once that is mastered, the concept is to channel your will into your projection to overtake someone else. Once you do, you will have control of them for a limited time, and in limited capacity. Anything to inflict self-harm will immediately shunt you out of their body. Now, taking over another being is also taxing on you, for you are effectively living in two bodies at once. It will be a considerable drain on you, especially depending on the state of the person."

"How do you mean?" Fiona asked, completely fixated on Fiona's explanation. "If they are in rough health, it will take less to actively sustain possession of them long-term, compared to someone in prime condition. However, this can also work against you, for the longer you remain in a weakened body, the more they'll begin to draw upon your own projection for strength. Another important thing to note is that the individual spirit and will of another, has a factor in how easily you can take over. Those in a more passive state of mind, weaker willed and with little self-awareness will be much easier to overtake. Those of strong consciousness, will and bearing will be much more difficult to possess. Also, the condition of sleep overall makes it much easier to do so as well."

"That makes sense," Fiona said as she stood up from her chair. "Oh, and lest I forget, you could also travel in astral form to seek other essence users out. It will take practice, like with all things. But you can travel in astral projection, which made things easier to prepare against other tribes. I could project and slip into other tribes without them noticing and learn of their plans to siege us. Our tribe could be forewarned from the reconnaissance I would embark on. I would also enter the dreams of the sleeping warriors and harass them with nightmares to shake their resolve."

"Now then, I'd like to learn how to astral project." Fiona said, doing little to hide her excitement.

 "Well then, it sounds like we've got work to do. Sarita replied. Let's get learning. I would like to find the others out there like me."

CHAPTER 5

AWAKENED BLOOD

When January rolled around, Sam was presented with the option to go on an archaeology trip with his class to Mexico. Not wanting to pass up such an opportunity, he gladly accepted, and together, the class made their way for the Aztec ruins of Teotihuacan from Colorado, as a lengthy road trip. Over the next two days, the class all drove in a convoy across the stretch of Mexico. Sam, never having quite visited before, felt right at home with the Hispanic culture that he grew up around back home in Hialeah. The scenery was a beautiful mix of cities and towns, desert, rocks, and dry air outside, cooled from the usual scorching heat due to the season. Sam was extremely excited to see history from so long ago up close and personal, and to learn more from a culture of the past. As he drove down the open road, his other classmates in the only other vehicles on the road with him, Hanska appeared next to him in the passenger seat and said, "Off to Teotihuacan, yes?"

"That we are, yes," Sam happily replied. "It's important to learn the history of cultures past. I'm happy that you enjoy such a thing."

"I absolutely love learning about history. Such untold gems of things, cultures of the past on display and more. What's not to love?" Hanska chuckled and said, "That's a good mindset to have. Whenever you have the opportunity, I would enjoy showing my old village as well where my tribe once lived."

"I would love to visit. From everything you told me about the Parduska clan, you all lived an interesting life. Freshly hunted and fished animals, navigation with stars, homebrewed drinks from the fruits in the forests, and of course the use of essences."

"Obviously, you live in a far more advanced culture from all that I've seen thus far. But yes, those were all things we had in the past. It was our way of life."

"You know what else from the past I'm curious about? Wyverns. I didn't think actual dragons existed. And yet, not only were the tales of the Dracosapiens true, but we ran into one the other day."

"Loxa. It was truly a sight to behold a wyvern up close."Hanska said.

"Did they exist in your time?" Sam inquired.

"We never actually encountered one. However, for a short time, I recall seeing them en masse with the Dracosapiens. That was before Rodrigo had split us all up." Sam shook his head and asked, "Why would he split you all up?"

"More numbers for the Jan Damis. He wanted his own society, something like we had in our tribe, but on a greater scale. Back then, he wanted sweeping conquest when he used the leopard ritual to create our essences. However, the village would not have him using our own. I and the others opposed him, sending him, the war chief and shadow master away in exile."

"Especially with what he did to your fiancée. That was horrible." Sam chipped in.

"Sam, there is nothing more I would like to do than end Rodrigo and avenge Marcela. I have the stirring feeling that somewhere down the line, we will cross paths again. And it will not end peacefully." Hanska replied.

"Hanska, whenever we do run into that scumbag again, I too would like to settle a score with him. He attacked the Sigma Pi house, hurt my brothers, and sent Bradley after Sara and me, endangering her. I have nothing but contempt for him." said Sam.

"Let's just hope that the other essence users aren't on Rodrigo's side as well." Hanska replied.

By evening, Sam had arrived at the hotel where his class was staying at, checked in and was looking for things to do. Down the road at one of the centers, there was a kickboxing event taking place and Sam decided it would be interesting to go see. He left the hotel and drove up the road for fifteen minutes before arriving at a pavilion of sorts that held events. Parking his car at the lot, Sam got out of the car and made his way to the front door where tickets were being sold. Taking some of the pesos he had on hand, Sam handed them to the entrance staff and made his way in. A long hall with several doors could be seen, along with the roaring of a crowd coming from the other end. Sam quickened his pace and jogged down the hall to arrive at a black double door. Pushing the metal handle in, Sam opened the door to see a ring, and rows of people cheering and shouting around it. There in the middle, were two kickboxers exchanging blows. One was wearing yellow shorts and blue gloves, the other was wearing black with red gloves. The young man in black shorts caught Sam's attention, from the sheer fighting ferocity he had. His tan skin and shoulder-length black hair seemed to mesh well with his strong, chiseled frame as he fought his opponent. Hanska appeared and said to Sam, "Sam, something is interesting about that man. His fighting spirit is very deadly and focused."

"Well, good thing that I'm not fighting him, and his opponent is. Let's go watch," Sam replied as he made his way for a seat. Sam made his way to the front row, where there was a seat available and took it. Sam felt the presence of the fighter in black shorts as he fought on, a knot forming in his stomach. The fighter in black shorts parried a few blows and slipped through other ones, before going on a counterattack. The announcer was speaking in Spanish, which Sam understood fluently and heard him say that the fighter in black shorts was an up-and-coming fighter named Diego Branco, hailing from Mexico. His opponent was from Canada, a blond-haired fighter named Tim, who was struggling to hold his own against the native. Diego's fists struck out with blinding speed, connecting in several spots, and sending Tim back against the ropes. The two clenched, and Tim ineffectively threw some knees at Diego to try and mount another offense against him, which only got him tossed across the ring. Tim tumbled and rolled back to his feet, the referee stepping in to let him regain his footing. Diego's eyes never left his opponent as Tim put his guard back up and referee signaled for the sight to resume. The crowd was chanting for Diego, cries of "Parduska!" sounding off in unison. "Leopard? Is that his ring nickname? What a name to have," Sam thought aloud as he watched on, completely drawn into the fight. Diego advanced and began another deadly assault, a mixture of punches and high kicks aimed at the head, clearly showing his intent to end the fight quickly. As he took a light jab, Diego furiously countered with a right that caught Tim in the jaw and staggered him back. Sam's eyes went wide when he thought he saw the faint glow of something red appear before Diego, as he charged forth to continue the attack. "Hanska, what did I just see?" Sam asked. "His spirit. Diego has a powerful will and spirit, which may have just manifested before us. He's certainly strong, that's for sure," Hanska replied. "…you don't think he's another essence user, do you?"

"He may very well be. It would make sense why the crowd calls him leopard. He may very well be another user. If that's the case, approaching him after this fight should be done carefully." Diego slipped past another punch and returned a right straight of his own, hitting the mark and snapping Tim's head back. Tim took a plummet to the mat and splayed out on it, motionless. The referee began the count, and got no response, ending the fight at six, waving his arms to the table where the bell was. The bell rung three times, and Diego was announced the winner of the fight. The referee raised his hand as the crowd roared in excitement, cheering for Diego. He was announced the champion as a woman came out and handed him a belt with a golden plate on it. Diego roared and raised his fist in the air, cheering with the crowd for his victory. The announcer took the mic and moved closer to Diego, then said, "Congratulations on your grand victory! Tell us, after such a hard-fought series of fights, how did you make it this far?"

"I have dreams of becoming a professional and fighting across the world. To have such dreams, I must be tough enough to not only fight for my country, but my family as well. This is something I'm truly passionate about, and I wouldn't trade it for anything in the world," Diego calmly replied, his deep voice belying his strength. The crowd roared yet again at his statement, then calmed down as the announcer asked, "Now that you have the title of Mexico in your grasp, I imagine your next fight is to take on the world. When would that be?"

"As soon as I can. My coach has already begun looking for fighters to take on the world stage. I have no doubt that the matches ahead will be interesting for sure. But I will do my best to make Mexico proud and put us on the map for serious world contenders in kickboxing, much like our boxers do." The crowd nearly tore the roof off with their rabid cries, going wild at Diego's words. "For such a strong fighter, he's very eloquently spoken and modest," Sam said, admiring the fighter who looked no older than he. "He has the heart of a warrior, through and through. At the very least, it would be good to meet and speak with him about his victory," Hanska added. Sam turned back to the ring to see Diego looking straight at him. Sam made eye contact and felt the strong presence from the ring as if it were right before him. Diego slowly turned around and headed with his coach back down the way to the locker room. Sam got up and said to Hanska, "We need to follow him. Why would he just stare us down like that?"

"I agree. There's shrinking doubt that he is indeed another user." Sam walked through the doors that led to the hall where fighters would go to their locker rooms. Surely enough, there was Diego, standing with his arms crossed, fully dressed, leaning against a wall. His eyes looked up to meet Sam's, as he said in his native tongue, "Do you speak Spanish?"

"It's my second language, yes," Sam replied in the same language.

"I see. Did you enjoy the fight?"

"Very much so. You're extremely skilled. However, I doubt that's why you had me come back here."

"So, you knew I was indeed calling you back here?" Diego said.

"That stare said it all. We may have a common ground that we share." Sam replied.

"I believe we do indeed. Tell me, can you see this?" Diego said as the red form of a leopard appeared before him.

"Clear as day," Sam replied. "I'm guessing you could see the same on me?"

"That blue figure of a man with you? Yes. I saw him out of the corner of my eye during the fight. That caught my attention. Tell me, do you know what it is?" Diego asked.

"How much do you know about the Parduska tribe?" Sam said, replying with a question of his own.

"Other than it's my epithet and this spirit with me now? Not much." Sam smiled and said to Diego, "Then why don't we go somewhere away from ears and eyes and have this conversation?" Diego got off the wall and beckoned for Sam to follow him into the locker room where he was before. Opening the door, his coach looked at the two with a confused expression. "It's okay, he's with me. Let us speak in private," Diego said. The coach complied and left the room, while Diego shut the door. The two young men sat down across from each other in the chairs there, as Sam offered his hand out. "Sam Cruz, a pleasure to meet you." Diego took his hand and replied, "Diego Branco. The pleasure is mine. Now then, what is this about, Sam?"

CHAPTER 6

IRON AND BLOOD

"So effectively, I now have the ability to turn into a leopard and use their latent abilities? That explains why my reflexes are faster now," Diego said, digesting Sam's explanation. "Exactly. And from what Hanska says, you are just like me. Though, I'm not sure if you've communed with your essence or not."

"If you mean tried to communicate with, I have on occasion. But I can't exactly have a conversation with a leopard."

"Your spirit is a leopard?" Sam said in surprise. Hanska appeared before the two and replied, "It's the blood beast. The blood beast essence isn't a normal human. It is the manifest spirit of the human sacrificed to mesh with the spirit of a leopard. The blood beast was a legendary hunter that excelled in battle and hunting others. It's no surprise you're a champion of Mexico."

"Does that mean the spirit has been helping me in my fights?" Diego asked.

"I would imagine so. But it is certainly not to take away from your already impressive skills. The essences have only been awakened for the past year or so."

"Well, that is certainly good to know. I was confused about why I suddenly felt like I had superpowers or something like that. Or maybe some brujeria was cast on me."

"It's not your fault you have it within. The essences choose the users."

"Well then, what brings you to Mexico, Sam?"

"I'm here with my class to research more on Teotihuacan. I'm studying archaeology with my college here." Diego nodded his head and replied, "I see. I'm glad that we crossed paths to better understand all of this. What should I do from here?"

"Meditate with your essence, learn from it more. Also, be warned of a man that may very well come for your life because you have it." Diego's eyes leveled with Sam as he replied, "And who may that be that wishes to challenge me?"

"A man named Rodrigo. He's the founder of the essences, the leopard king. Do not let him sway you to his cause if he finds you.

He wishes to bring the essences under his command and begin a
society anew like he did before."

"The Jan Damis, from what you told me? No man subjugates me,
period. I'm a proud fighter of the Branco family. We kneel to no
man." Sam smiled at the resolve in Diego's heart and replied,
"That's the way it should be, Diego. No man should bow to
another." It was Diego's turn to smile at the sentiment, and said, "I
like you, Sam. How long are you going to be in Mexico for?"

"A good two weeks or so."

"I would like to meet up again before you leave."

"I think we can certainly arrange for that."

Over the next two weeks, Sam would split his time between field
studies of the ruins and occasionally meeting up with Diego. The
studies at the ruins were mesmerizing to Sam. He was enamored
by the history and lore of the Aztec gods, and the culture of the
Aztecs. Sam found tablets and pictures of people that were
standing next to leopards, and wondered if the Jan Damis were
blended into the Aztec people when they came up from Peru. The
archaeology professor explained that the depictions indeed spoke
of people that were believed to be able to shift into leopards and
back, which only confirmed Sam's suspicions of the Jan Damis
and their spread around the world. When classes weren't being
held at the ruins, Sam would meet up with Diego and the two
would go sightseeing the city at night. Diego would also have Sam
get in sparring practices with him, in response to Sam expressing a
desire to become better at combat. Sam was outright impressed
with Diego's skill: not only was he naturally talented and trained
from a young age, but the essence he had, only helped grow his
own talents. Sam trained plenty with Hanska, and gained a decent
competitive edge with his own skills, but fell short of what Diego
could do. Regardless, Sam was grateful for it and took the
teaching in stride, adding it to his own collective knowledge base,
so that it could help him in future encounters. When they would
finish, Sam would bring Hanska out to show Diego how to
meditate and commune with the essence within, bridging the gap
between essence and user. Diego would commune with the blood
beast inside him, and he could feel a primal energy and instinct
heighten within. Hanska took extra time to help Diego bond with
the red leopard in him, for it was not a conventional essence. Most

were human and could speak with their bearer, but not so much the blood beast. Diego couldn't quite grasp what the blood beast would tell him, for the large cat would only growl, purr, or roar. However, he began to feel its emotions and sentiments from simply being around him, watching his body language, and feeling what the cat felt. Diego and Sam would also practice using their essences to interact in their place.

One night, when they had finished bringing both essences out, Hanska said, "There's another essence user here. We must be careful." Sam and Diego stood up, and Diego asked, "Do they wish us harm?"

"I don't believe so, but that doesn't mean we just lower our guard so easily." Two young men walked in, and Hanska said to the others, "They have essences, but none that I have ever seen before. Something is not right here." The blood beast began to growl, and Diego felt a pull in his gut, something not feeling right. "I don't think the guys here mean us well. We had best prepare for a confrontation," he said, standing up, ready to intercept the two. Both young men were dressed in suits, one with cropped blond hair, and one with light brown. "Ah, I see we found our mark," the brown haired one said. "And who are you?" Sam asked, reverted to English language to answer them. "We're here to retrieve our friend here."

"Retrieve? How do you mean?" asked Sam.

"We're going to take him back with us to our boss. He's of need to him."

Diego, English being his second language, understood what both were saying. He chose to only speak Spanish with Sam as a sign of shared culture, and decided to play dumb as he shrugged his shoulders. Sam, catching on to the ploy, started speaking in Spanish to him, and Diego nodded, feigning his ignorance of the matter before responding. "Well, what did he say?" the brown haired one asked.

"He said you have no business here and should leave." Sam replied.

"That's going to be a problem, for our boss has paid us to come retrieve him."

"I don't think your boss would be so unreasonable as to resort to abduction, now would he? Who is your boss, anyways?" Sam asked. "Our boss is none of your concern, except that he is simply wanting to bring this guy back. How he comes back is his choice, as long as he's alive." Diego's eyes lit up as he balled his hands into fists and began cracking his knuckles. Sam replied, "Well, it sounds like a threat to us. But if you insist on trying to take him, you'll have to take me on too." The two young men in suits immediately shifted into leopards and charged Diego and Sam. Diego, his instincts already on high alert, dodged the feline missile of mass and threw a roundhouse kick into its sides, sending it crashing into the wall. Sam turned into his leopard form as well and ducked under the other leopard, springing up and smashing into his underside, knocking him up in the air. Sam then sprung off his powerful hind legs, raked his claws into the leopard and slammed him back down to the floor. The leopard bounced with a thud and scrambled to get back to his feet. Sam wasted little time in using the leopard's disorientation to charge ahead and tackle him, successfully doing so through a table nearby. Sam shifted back into human form and shuffled back, his fists already up. "You have the option to quit. Don't press your luck," Sam warned. The leopard, clumsily regaining his footing, made another attempt to charge Sam. Sam sidestepped out of the way as the leopard smashed into a metal support pole that went up to the ceiling, then rolled on the ground. Another leopard went flying across near Sam as he saw Diego moving after it in his human form, having yet to shift. The leopard had little time to recover to his feet, as Diego grabbed it by the scruff of his neck with two hands, and drove a series of knee strikes into its ribs. A sickening crack was heard, and Sam could tell Diego must've broken the shifter's ribs. He then threw it against the wall and pinned it down by the neck. Diego, his face now savagely enraged, threw the ploy of playing dumb out the window, growled at the shifter and said, "I'll give you a chance to get out of this gym." His eyes began to glow red and Sam felt the air nearby grow heavy as he saw the red glow of the leopard from Diego snarl at the shifter. A presence of malicious, violent intent began to fill the room, giving the other shifter cause to turn back into his human form and run in sheer terror. "If you choose to remain and fight, I will crush you utterly. Your friend has already fled. I will not give you another chance to leave after that. Any threat to me or my friends are met with swift vengeance. If you still want a battle, then let us fight to the death," Diego warned. Sam even had to remember to breathe, for such was the presence Diego had, that it seemed to choke off the air in the room. "Hanska, what is happening?" Sam asked. "Diego's will is manifesting. Not only is the blood beast a powerful entity alone, but Diego's own will and spirit are strong as well. His spirit with the essence is simply enacting and dominating with will alone," Hanska replied. The shifter switched back to human form and whined while coughing blood out, "Please! Don't! I'll leave!" Diego pulled the young man to his feet, kicked him in the rear and cried, "Then get out!" The young man followed where his companion left and hurried out the door, not thinking twice on trying to stay. The air began to return to normal again as Diego said to Sam, "We got them out of here. Are you okay?"

"Yes. Yourself?" Sam replied, gathering his composure again. "I feel fantastic. What a fight, and against leopards! I'll be sure to skin one if we're attacked again."

"Hanska, where did they get their essences from? I thought we were the only ones already in the world?" Sam asked. "Those weren't of the original five. Either Rodrigo has now split essences again, or he's making new ones. I'm not sure on which as of now," Hanska responded. Looking to Diego, he added, "By the way, you've displayed a great ability in your will projection. This is something I would like to further train you both on." "I did?" Diego replied, puzzled.

"Yes. Come. Let us meditate on what happened and I'll begin to explain how to do so." Sam and Diego were sitting across from each other as Hanska appeared before them. "Enacting your will over another is one of two things I'd like to teach. The other is using your manifested essence to battle for and with you. Sam, you're familiar with this in our previous lessons, where you and I have battled in the woods before. But we'll begin with the former." The red leopard appeared before the two and sat next to Hanska, flicking its tail, and purring as Hanska continued, "The dominance of will is something anyone has access to. Humans since the dawn of time have put their will into action, and it is not limited to any one person. However, not all are cognizant of that. To truly make it effective, one must be of purpose. One must be of power and strength; once those are in line, your own will can dominate another's with great effectiveness."

"That's pretty much what Diego did then, huh," Sam added. Diego nodded his head and replied, "I take great honor in my fighting ability and to not be brought down by another. I'm on a path to be able to help my family out and make sure they will be okay. Being brought down here is inexcusable."

"Exactly the necessary mentality required to employ such dominance," Hanska explained. "Sam, you too can achieve this with practice. Diego happens to not only be a natural at it, but has a furious drive within to lead him to do so. His mentality and will are strong, born from a need to change his life around from desperation and anger." The red leopard seemed to nod at such a notion and let out a small roar.

"What about the second thing you wanted to teach us?" Diego asked. "Manifesting your essence. This is like enacting your will, but instead focusing on giving energy to your essence to either fight alongside you, or for you. This is extremely effective in avoiding direct battles, for only your mental energy is needed to control an essence. Using your essence while you yourself are in a battle, is much harder versus standing back and letting the essence battle on your behalf. An essence can cause psychological and spiritual damage, and make it seem as if they are alive and hitting you. What's really happening is the spirit and will are being attacked, as well as the mind firing off the pain receptors from each blow." Hanska walked up to Diego and chopped his forearm, to which Diego found himself reeling from the blow. Yet there was no bruise or lasting damage. "That is beyond words…" Diego said with amazement, beginning to think of all he could do with the red leopard in fights outside of the ring. "You have a naturally high disposition to not being dominated, so you would do exceptionally well to learn this," Hanska explained. "In real life encounters with other essence users, you could send the blood beast to fight them in your place and not even move a muscle. However, that takes a great deal of calming the mind, and an attunement to your essence. Sam would have a much easier time with this since his mind stays clear, has a deeper attunement with me, and thinks on his feet. Not to say that you do not, Diego, it's just that you simply have more leaning towards wielding strength and sharp reflexes."

"Essentially, I have more animal instinct while Sam has more of a disposition to think his way out of things. That makes sense, for I do prefer to handle things with my fists," Diego chuckled. "But it makes sense to me. I would like to practice it."

"Very good. I feel that both of you could stand to learn manifestation first. The will domination would translate better afterwards, so we'll start with that. To begin, you both will channel your essences, which would be myself and the blood beast over there, into battling on your behalf. Use your thoughts to envision all you'd like us to, then do it." Sam and Diego got up from the floor and made their way across from each other. "Well then, this will be fun," Sam said as he brought out Hanska in front of him, focusing on Hanska following his every thought. "I've never done this before, but I certainly like it," Diego replied, summoning out the blood beast before him. Hanska and the red leopard both took fighting poses, while the two young men simply watched and focused on their respective manifested essence. "All right, let's see what you got, Diego!" Sam chimed as Hanska charged forth. Diego nodded in kind as the red leopard pounced forth to meet the iron spiritualist. The two met in a clash and began to fight with one another, Hanska using intricate footwork to keep the leopard off-balance. The red leopard swiped a few times and missed the blue glowing man, before getting knocked away with a backfist. Diego felt a jarring sensation in his mind and continued to focus, but could tell that he had already made a slip up that would cost him. Hanska continued to deliver blow after blow, staggering Diego's focus with each hit. At a point, the red leopard dissipated and Diego had to defog his mind, which had grown hazy from the battle.

"Taking damage in battle like that will rattle your focus. Your mind must always be solid and calm. You have a propensity to give into rage in combat, which isn't bad at all for you. However, maintaining your essence is a different matter," Hanska explained. Diego nodded and felt his mind clear up as he replied, "That is incredible. Hanska, thank you for your guidance. I'm learning invaluable things because of you, as well as getting to know my essence better." The red leopard reappeared next to Diego, seemingly unfazed from the fight and licked its paw, then growled at Diego. "He said he doesn't want to be known as just the blood beast. He wants a name," Diego said, surprised he understood the leopard.

"You can understand him now? It means you must be closer to him already," Hanska applauded. "Well then, my friend, how about Rojo? For your proud color and spirit?" Diego asked. The leopard purred and nodded its head, which brought grins of approval from Sam and Hanska. "Very well, then you are Rojo, the proudest leopard to have ever been in my eyes," Diego replied. Rojo got up and slunk around Diego's leg, rubbing his head and body along his shin. "For such a strong animal, he certainly is cute," Sam quipped, admiring the leopard's affection. Hanska walked over to Rojo and put out a hand, which Rojo happily met and nudged. "My, you must've been a proud beast in life. It's sad that Rodrigo did this to you so many years ago, but now you are with someone who fights as fiercely as you. Two leopards of the same spots. You were one of the two main essences that weren't part of our tribe, but I welcome you all the same, Rojo," Hanska calmly said with a smile on his face. Rojo gave a small meow in between purrs, understanding Hanska quite well as a fellow kindred essence, and as a being. "Well then, I say we continue practicing and getting good at this," Diego said. "There's much more I wish to learn, and if I'm going to be sought out by some people, they won't be taking me without a fight."

CHAPTER 7

OMEN OF A GATHERING

"Oh dear, that does present a problem for us," Mr. Viejas said over the phone outside of a casino. "Not only is he the essence user, but also has Sam's help? Things have become more complicated indeed. Do not pursue them anymore for now. No need to risk your well-being when they've proven themselves superior. Stay focused on them and keep an eye on their movements." Hanging up the phone, a curious Fiona dressed in a green evening dress asked, "What happened?"
"Nothing to worry about. Our fellow associates ran into some trouble while seeking out some friends of ours, but all is handled," Mr. Viejas replied, tipping his brimmed fedora to her with a mercurial smile. He knew that if he told her the reality of things, Fiona would likely become unsettled. The fact of the essences existing and the company ultimately starting a new order like the Jan Damis of old days, coupled with the experience she had in Japan would likely cause a rift. Mr. Viejas knew subtlety and misdirection was key when it was called for. "Oh. Well, that's good I suppose. Are you ready to hit the tables?" Mr. Viejas chuckled and replied, "I was born for tables and chance. Let us head inside and I'll show you how I initially earned money." The night sky hung over the two as the lights from the casino shone brilliantly in a cascade of colors, the steps leading up to it only further intensifying the atmosphere. The two headed up the steps and walked through the sliding doors where more colors, and various sounds of voices, slot machines, and music mixed in a revelry of controlled madness, all joined together to capture the essence of gamblers and goers in one building. Fiona looked around in awe, having never been to a casino before, and looked to see Mr. Viejas's eyes light up with attentive passion. His glance focused on a table ahead. She had never really seen that look in his eyes before, not until now, and could see he was deeply passionate about his craft. He beckoned with a nod for them to approach the table, striding cross the plush purple carpet to the table. There was a trio of players there, each one down on their chips and luck from what their body language showed. Mr. Viejas

pulled out a chair for Fiona, then sat down himself to the right end of the table and warmly said to the dealer, "Ah, good evening my friend!"

"And a good evening to you, sir," the dealer warmly replied. "Joining in?"

Mr. Viejas pulled out ten one hundred-dollar bills and slid them across the table. "As long as the face cards keep coming and the twenty-one keeps hitting," he jovially replied, prompting a chuckle from the other players. The dealer took the bills, smashed them into the slot with the acrylic pusher, then pulled the correct amount of chips out to give to Mr. Viejas. Taking half of his stack, he slid them over to Fiona. "I've never played blackjack before," Fiona said, looking at the stack of brightly colored chips. "No need. You'll pick up in due time easily," Mr. Viejas replied. Fiona looked behind the dealer to see a shadowy form that looked exactly like Mr. Viejas appear out of thin air. The form held a thumbs up with a friendly smile, and Fiona realized they would have a much greater edge against the table with whatever Mr. Viejas could do. The cards were dealt, and Mr. Viejas's eyes would scan each one on the table, as well as the shoe and the discard pile. "Hm, a ten and a three. Not the best way to start, but I'll manage," he quipped to himself, while he switched his sight to his shadow double. His next card would be a seven if he hit. "Dealer, how well has this table been?" Mr. Viejas asked.

"Are you kidding? I couldn't even get a face card for the last ten hands if I dealt it myself!" one of the other men replied in frustration.

"It's been kind of bad for the players. Maybe you'll change it up," the dealer excitedly replied, trying to play into building excitement for the players.

"Thirteen there. Tough call on that one. Book says hit, but you could always stay and make me potentially bust." said the dealer.

"Hm…well now, if I'm to bring in a new wave luck, that means taking chances, no?" Mr Viejas replied.

"That is one way to shift luck. But who knows? A rain dance might do the same thing!" Mr. Viejas nodded slowly and began circling his right index finger while glaring at his cards, then made a show of replying, "Very good! Then tempt fate, we shall! I'd like to double down!"

"A double down on thirteen? Are you sure, sir?" the dealer asked, bewildered but amused.

"I am. We need to shake things up at this table, and dammit if I don't arrive with some flare!" The dealer dealt to his hand, and the seven arrived, which caused the dealer and the other players to look with widened eyes, and establish the beginning of smiles upon the players faces.

"A twenty! Well then mister, that was well played!" the dealer exclaimed.

"Holy crackers, this man has balls!" one of the players added, the mood of the table beginning to lighten. Fiona looked to the dealer, moving on to her after Mr. Viejas waved his hand to stay. With a two and a queen, her glance caught the shadowy form now right behind the dealer, making the hand gesture to hit twice, then stay.

"Hit," Fiona called. A six came out on the table. "Eighteen. A good spot to land," said the dealer.

"I'll push my luck a bit here. Hit again," Fiona said. A three hit the table.

"Goodness, twenty-one!" the dealer said. "You guys just brought some luck to the table here!"

"Can't have any fun if we're not winning, right?" Mr. Viejas teased, keeping the atmosphere light, and his presence innocent to the table. They had no idea just how much he and Fiona were going to take from their establishment that night. Fiona, having never played before, immediately felt a thrill from the first hand, and coupled with Mr. Viejas, she had an even better feeling she wasn't going to lose either.

****

In a darkened room lit by torches and candlelight, a group of young men and women were gathered around, while a cloaked figure stepped out to a stone altar. Against the wall, there was a line of various men, each in orange jumpsuits and with bags over their heads. The candles flickered and danced ominously, while the young men and women in the audience had gathered around to watch the cloaked figure speak.

"All of you have been summoned here to gain the next step of ascendancy," the cloaked figure spoke, in a man's voice, with arms waving out to the crowd. "You all have been handpicked to join the inner group, to take the next step to realizing your full self. Now, I understand this would look rather horrific to the uninitiated, but you all understand what is at hand here."

"These are hapless criminals, spared from death row so you can do the honors instead: let them meet their punishment!" one young man cried, with the crowd chanting their agreement.

"Indeed, they are. But instead of wasting life, we are using theirs to better ours. With what will transpire here, they will surrender their life energy to you, so that you may achieve greater heights of potential from beyond. You've all seen what I can do as is, and now is the time for you all to obtain the same. What started as merely business to aid all of you on the next step of your life, will now ingrain you to become your own tribe. To this end, we will conquer!"

The crowd of the college students cheered in glee, for they had seen what the man in the cloak could do. They couldn't refuse the money he paid them, nor his abilities. A sane person would normally think such claims of both were impossible, but this man showed just how real those things were. The cloaked man grabbed one of the inmates along the walls and dragged him by his manacles to the altar. He groaned as he was pulled up to the stone top and made to lie down atop it. The flames on the torches and candles began to flicker and dance, as if responding to the prisoner's impending fate. The cloaked man began chanting something in an ancient dialect of Spanish, unbeknown to the participants bearing witness to the ritual. The chant started in a low voice, with a slow cadence that gradually rose in volume and pace, with each repeat of the lines. The air began to grow thick and heavy, a weighted power started to form in the room. The young men and women began to look at one another with side glances of apprehension, unsure of what was to happen next. A dull thrumming could be felt in the air, and the flames from any light sources started to turn an eerie green, full of ancient power. The cloaked man drew a knife from his sleeve and ran his hand across the blade. As he did, a slew of runes began to glow the same color as the flames on it, following the man's touch as it caressed the blade. The other prisoners on the wall began to shake and tremble with fear, not knowing what was happening outside of the hoods they were forced to wear. The man on the altar squirmed, writhing as if pinned down by some invisible force. Try as he did, he could not move from the spot he was pinned down to. "What…what is this?!" he cried a muffled question from out of his hood.

"The tethers of power now have you. Unless I will it, you cannot escape from here," the cloaked man coolly replied, brandishing the blade. A hand pulled the hood off the prisoner, and a panicked face looked into the shadow of the cloaked hood where a face should have been. A pair of catlike green eyes stared back in the darkness, prompting the man to scream. "NO! Please, don't let me go out like this!" the man cried, tears starting to stream down his face. "But we freed you from your execution in that prison!" the cloaked man replied. "You see, your captors were so kind as to strike a deal where we could take all of those slated for death. We are going to make far better use of you and your friends than the prison ever could." The man slowly raised the knife up, now glowing with power, as the prisoner began mumbling a prayer to himself, completely overtaken by fear. A moment of silence fell over the room, as everyone watched the man pause with his arms over his head, before swiftly driving the knife down into the prisoner's chest. A choking sound came from him, and blood began to pool around the wound. His eyes lost all light and life as his body began to glow with the outline of green. His face was contorted and frozen in agony, his last thoughts and emotions painted clearly on his face. The runes shone brightly, making the knife seem almost alive with its own power. Once the light had swirling round the body moved to the knife, the weapon itself turned bright green. The cloaked man removed the knife from the prisoner's chest and held it up to the now silent crowd for all to see. Chanting another incantation, the knife glowed once again. Teeming with power, the cloaked man pointed it to the crowd and the knife shot forth a beam of light that forked into three, slamming into the chests of two young women and one male, and knocking them off their feet. They writhed in agony on the floor for a moment, while the others looked on with rapt attention. After what seemed like an eternity, the trio stood back up to their feet, breathing hard and inspecting their bodies. A faint glow of green outlined them, and their eyes briefly narrowed into cat-like slits, before returning to normal and garnering the undivided attention and surprise of the others. "My friends, this is the dawning of your awakening," the cloaked man said to the crowd with arms outstretched. "We will all become brothers and sisters of the Parduska Clan. We will become the only and last living inheritors of true power!" The crowd erupted in rapturous applause, calling for the next prisoner to be sacrificed to bestow more power to them. The cloaked man smiled and said to himself aloud, "Once our numbers are numerous again, we can begin searching for the remnant soul of the rival clan's leader, the jaguar king, the only other man that stood against me even I after I left the Leopard Clan. Unfortunately for him, he was the only one of his kind to exist as a shifter. If I can find and obtain his power, then we will truly begin anew, and be even better than the Jan Damis of yore." All the college students watched the trio adjust to their newfound abilities of heightened senses and reflexes, and were mesmerized. The clamor only kept growing as each one wanted to be next in line to gain powers. "Now, now," the cloaked man reassured everyone, "We have nothing but time tonight to make sure everyone receives the gift of the tribe. Besides, no need to rush such a grand display of power transference, right? Let us savor the gift that awaits you all and soak in such magnificence!"

****

 Fiona and Mr. Viejas were walking away from the chip counter where gamblers could cash in winnings. Mr. Viejas was brushing the green, crisp bills with his thumb, letting the flapping noise ring through the air. A whole slew of other banded amounts were tucked away in a violet leather bag he carried. "Well Miss Fiona, I do believe we walked away with two million and some change from that one. One of the best hauls, I must say," Mr. Viejas chimed happily with a satisfied grin on his face. "I can't believe that! So much in one night!" Fiona exclaimed in euphoric disbelief. "Now I know what you may be thinking, and yes: I did pull money like this before I ever obtained my essence. I relied on card counting much more before I had my shadow ability, but even with that, I still use the card count to keep track of what goes on." "How many times have you used your ability with a partner?" "Honestly, with another? This is a first. I used to have a small team of friends where we all had different roles in scouting a table out to pick on and take money from, before I ever had my essence."

"Really? What was that like?" Fiona asked as the two made their way to a limousine taxi Mr. Viejas had called. The two slid onto a buttery leather seat, with a decanter of bourbon and glasses ready on the other side. The door closed and the driver made his way to the wheel and began driving. "It was fun, intricate, and thrilling," Mr. Viejas said, staring off ahead into recollection. His eyes and face lit up with excitement, much more than his usual amused expression. "There were three of us. Each of us knew how to count and play well enough, but I was usually the star player to bring it home. Jack was what we called our temp checker. He would read a dealer and a table, and get a count on the cards of how the table was doing. Clark would join the table first and set the table up for the sweep. Once they were in place, I'd come in and together, we'd all work the table and take everything we could from them."

"Did the casinos ever catch on to you three?" Fiona asked.

"They would back us off from time to time, but we had the act of being strangers down so much, our banter would not only amuse others on the table, but could stand to be on par with television show writing!"

Fiona took a glass that Mr. Viejas had poured for her as he quaffed some of the fine bourbon himself. "Ah, smoky and mellow: my favorite!" he spoke with a smile.

"And so, you would make a living simply hitting casinos to take them for whatever you could win from them?"

"Yes. In my younger years, I would go no less than twenty times a year. I started putting my money towards investments and eventually scaled down my travel a bit. However, when I had my team, those were some of my highest earning trips. Granted, we split the winnings three ways, but it still was incredible. Not only was I pulling in money, but so were the other two. Collectively, we could amass much more. Once we earned our first million together, that was when I knew that the sky was the limit."

"Still, a million dollars is a lot of money!" Fiona exclaimed. "I hadn't even dreamt of seeing that much money until tonight!"

"It is very elating the first time, that's for sure. I guess when you see it more and more, you either get complacent with it, or you push to new levels."

"That makes sense. What happened to your team?" Mr. Viejas paused, and looked ahead with a small smile on his face. He took a pensive sip of his bourbon before answering. "Well," he began slowly, "Sadly, they died. Jack and Clark both went to a yacht party, while I stayed home to court a young lady I was seeing at the time. Unfortunately, there was a sudden storm that hit. The yacht was caught in the storm and attempted to make the voyage back to land. However, it was not to be. The yacht was well out to sea: not too far from home, but still miles enough where returning to shore would be no easy feat. The next day, search and rescue found the yacht capsized, and the bodies of all goers in the sea."
"Oh…I'm so sorry…I didn't mean to bring it up… That's tragic…I'm sorry to hear that." Fiona said with a long face.
"It's fine. Speaking of the memories with them would make them happy. They wouldn't want me to be silent on their lives," Mr. Viejas warmly replied, a low tone of grit mixed in with his voice. Mr. Viejas then sighed and replied, "I'm grateful I got to know such men and call them my friends. I carry with them their memory and try to make them proud with my life. That is the joy of life: to achieve something noteworthy, establish a legacy, and go forth into prosperity with a smile. Life goes on, and so do we."

CHAPTER 8

INTO THE SKIES

Within the month, Sam had returned with his schoolmates from his trip back to the campus, in which he was somewhat glad to be back. He did miss being down in Mexico with Diego, and made sure to give him his phone number before leaving, so the two could keep up with one another, and stay informed on any moves that Rodrigo's group would make. Sara and Fred were both ecstatic to see Sam return, and when they had settled down in the place that Sam and Fred stayed at, he informed the two of all that happened on his trip. "You mean to tell us there's more of these things now? Not just a select few?" Fred asked, his eyes lit with concern. Sara, more understanding and learned of the history of the Jan Damis, added, "If that's the case, we all could be in big danger. After all, if more are being made, it will only be a matter of time until things get terrible. And from what happened last year, Rodrigo and Mr. Viejas know we all go here." Sam nodded as he took a sip of his water and agreed, "It's a problem, all right. Only consolation is that we found the blood beast in Diego, who I'm friends with. I need to plan something to go hunt down Rodrigo and stop him from making anymore shifters. We're effectively sitting ducks on campus out here, while he has his location unknown to us. Who's to say he won't stop sending more of them after us?"

"Should we get Diego here?" Fred asked, leaning forward, and looking at Sam. Sam sighed and responded, "It would certainly help, but I'm not going to call Diego here simply to stand and watch. He has a life to live too, not to mention an upcoming title fight for him. I will probably get more information on things before forming something concrete with him. My immediate concern is making sure Sigma Pi and everyone else we know is safe."

"How many original essence users are there?" Sara inquired. "Six?"

"Yes. Bradley was the war chief that was sealed away in the Oro Luna. That leaves me, Diego, Rodrigo, and two unknowns. Hanska is going to teach me more of the meditation that helps an essence user find others. Apparently, Rodrigo is the best at it, though his reach is limited over vast distances. Hanska told me there's an artifact of the clan that can channel the essence and focus of someone, and magnify it, making it much easier to locate across such distances."

"Any idea where it may be?" Sara asked, her eyes widening with interest. Sam shook his head and replied, "Sadly not. We could use such a thing at a time like this. Not knowing who the other two are, as well as where these new shifters are coming from, is quite unsettling."

Fred got up from the couch and replied, "Not much we can do for now. However, I'll relay the information to the guys so that they're not caught unawares. That's the best thing I can do on this end at least. You're the expert on this stuff now in terms of shifters by nature, and with Sara knowing the history. If there's anyone that will figure things out, it will be you. I'll catch you later after talking with the Sigma Pi house." Fred headed out the doorway and got in his vehicle, taking off to go speak with the others. Meanwhile, Sara moved closer to Sam on the couch and grasped his hand. "If it's any help, I'll ask my grandpa if he knows of anything to help us deal with this," Sara said with a tone of concern. Sam rubbed the back of her hand, smiled, and replied, "That would help quite a bit, actually. I would accompany you to go see Ed, but I'm best left to focus on learning to locate better, via meditation." Sara nodded and kissed him before also getting up to leave the dorm cabin. As she headed out the door, she said to Sam, "If you need anything, feel free to call or head over." The door closed and soon the rumble of her vehicle was heard, followed by the tires grinding down the gravel and heading to the road, then away. Sam lit a candle and turned off the lights, preparing to meditate as he did when he was alone. He began to fall into his usual state in the beginning, focusing on his anchor and feeling the presence of Hanska appear next to him. The familiar outline of the tribe member then appeared in his mind to him, then knelt in front of him amidst the darkness of his mind.

"Very good, Sam. Relax. Let your mind become open, receptive to the world around you. Focus on the essence within. Let it be your lens in which you look through to the world, and may it help act to find others. Feel the essences out in the world." Sam felt the pull of his own essence in the pit of his chest, a slight tingling sensation of an invisible link being established over a great stretch of nothingness.

"I can feel the faint presence of another essence like mine somewhere out there. I'm not sure where, but it's out there," Sam quietly said. The feeling began to multiply, as though another link were being formed. Then another, and yet another, as more began to establish connection with him. The tingling sensation grew stronger, and the connections felt like they were moving.

"Hanska…are they getting closer?" Sam asked.

"No. These aren't shifters, at least these new connections. Something is different about them," Hanska replied, a hint of caution in his voice. Sam broke the meditative state he was in and felt the connections fade away. Yet, in its place, the feeling of being watched was there. Nerves on edge, Sam got up and slowly made his way to the window. He pulled down one of the blinds a bit with a finger and peered outside. There, sitting some distance away, was a large dark figure that easily made a human being look small. "What…what is that?" Sam asked. As if hearing and answering his question on cue, the shadow outside spoke in a loud voice, "Sam. It is Loxa. If you are here, "I've need to speak with you." Sam, surprised but also somewhat eased, grabbed his jacket and headed outside, also grabbing his camping lantern on the way. The light illuminated the darkness from night as it began to shine on the scaly figure of the wyvern. "Loxa…you scared the daylights out of me," Sam sighed. "What brings you back, let alone in the open sight of humans?"

"Something of importance. I have spoken with the other wyverns, and they wish to meet you," Loxa replied in his deep voice.

"I see…where are they?" Sam asked, unsure of what to make of the situation. Loxa looked up, signaling Sam to turn his gaze to the other figures that were flying around above.

"There's…more of them…"

"Yes. They had followed me to come see who you were for themselves. They didn't know a Jan Damis existed that fought for humanity, instead of trying to destroy them. They want to see if you are as much for the wyverns as well."

"Very well. What must I do?"

"Climb on to my back. I will take you up to the skies above, and we will have court with the wyverns up there." Sam, trusting the words of Loxa, climbed on and up to where the base of Loxa's neck was. With several powerful wing beats, Sam felt his stomach sink from the feeling of weightlessness, as the two took to the air and ascended for the stars. Loxa and Sam arrived atop the screen of a stretch of clouds, where Sam could make out the other figures of flying wyverns circling about, stopping their pattern to fly in place and encircle Loxa. Sam felt rather much out of his element and quite vulnerable, being surrounded by flying wyverns a rough thousand feet above the ground. Effectively an aerial captive to the audience before him. As the wyverns all steadied their flight in place, one with black skin and scales flew towards Loxa and Sam, with Sam's leopard-enhanced vision kicking in.

"Greetings, and well met, essence bearer. I am Tormarth," the black wyvern said with powerful resonance and grit in his tone. "We are the leaders of various wyvern groups around the world, or more of what is left of them. The Jan Damis, our sworn enemies from millennia back, hunted our numbers down greatly. With their advent return, we need to know of your intentions."

"Hello, Tormarth," Sam nervously replied, regaining his bearings in the process. "I'm Sam Cruz, and I am indeed one of the holders of the essences. I did not awaken, nor receive these powers willingly. I'm sure Loxa has informed you that one night on Mount Elbert, the Oro Luna set the original essences back into the world. I have battled one of the users, defeated him, and sealed away his power, for he threatened humanity with Rodrigo."

"Ah yes, the leopard king himself," Tormarth spat in disgust. "He led thousands of the Jan Damis to find and destroy us. You see, their abilities let them find our hideouts and slay us to the last wyrm. They saw us as threats to their ultimate reign and power, being another creature race of power." Sam cleared his throat and spoke during a pause of silence,

"And that's where the Dracosapiens helped."

"You know of the Dracosapiens?"

"The alliance between wyvern and man that crushed the Jan Damis? I do. I know of the members of the DuMont lineage that was close friends with Sir Ricard Vel. Illixus, the battles across the world, and the Oro Luna sealing away the fractured essences? I know of it all."

"How we can trust one human that knows so much of our history, without using it to wipe us out?" another one of the wyverns in the circle hissed. Tormarth nodded, let a moment of silence pass, then replied, "It is true that you do indeed know the history. How can we trust that you will not lead more to finish us off, let alone be with the others?" Sam replied with the utmost confidence that held an undercurrent of anger, "Because Rodrigo nearly had my girlfriend and I killed by one of his subordinates. Just a few weeks ago, I met another one of the essence users, and we took on Rodrigo's forces. Dealing with him and whatever new group he's making is enough for me. I have no cause or reason to extend my fight to the wyverns." Tormarth flew closer and stared Sam in the face, his orange eyes meeting Sam's, and beginning to glow. "I have the ability to discern intent and the bearing of a living being to some extent with my eyes, from my lineage of ancestry. If you are telling the truth, the other wyverns will see the glow of a white aura around you through me. If you lie and hold malice, then your aura will be purple. Ready to be judged?" Sam, driven by pure conviction and assured in his intentions, nodded and said, "Cast your gaze on me. Let the aura speak the truth, then." Tormarth's eyes glowed brighter, the two smoldering orange orbs glowing like flames in the night as he looked upon Sam. After a tense moment of silence, a glowing white aura appeared around Sam, drawing the gasps, and hushed surprised whispers of the others. "You…you indeed speak the truth…" Tormarth slowly replied, also taken aback. "Never in my lifetime did I think that one of the Jan Damis would indeed seek to protect life beyond their own…but your soul is committed to your will."

"I have no reason to even consider killing such great creatures," Sam replied honestly and warmly, his gaze not leaving Tormarth. "I only wish to stop Rodrigo and be rid of these essences, if such a thing is possible for the latter part. Listen Tormarth, Rodrigo is somehow growing his numbers again. I have allies on my side, but they are too few to do anything if Rodrigo bolsters his numbers beyond anything I can do. I would want the wyverns to help fight alongside me if that is of course okay with you. I wouldn't be so foolish to speak for a powerful being like you."

"Then Loxa was indeed telling the truth the whole time," Tormarth said aloud to the others. "For that, we are sorry to not only you, but to you as well, Sam. If this is such a crisis that is on the rise, then we would be honored to act in good faith and alliance like the humans and my kin did so many years ago. And this time, fortune would have it that we have an essence user on our side!" The other wyverns roared a cheer of sorts out, agreeing with Tormarth. Sam's face lit up with joy; his spirits boosted by the willingness of the wyverns to help.

"Tormarth…Loxa…all of you…thank you so much for lending your help. I thought that I was going to have to find a way on my own. I too have many loved ones I want to defend, and if that means I can help protect you all as well, then I'll fight for you too."

"Then let it be known on this night, that we will reinstate and bring to life once again, the alliance of the Dracosapiens in modern times. You have proven yourself a trustworthy ally in what seems to be a great battle to come."

"You also have a friend in me," Sam added. "Don't feel like a stranger if you ever wanted to have conversation or time together, I like making new friends, after all." The other wyverns roared again and began circling around Loxa and Tormarth, before taking off in single file across the sky. Tormarth also followed them, with Loxa picking up bearing and speed behind them.

"Whoa! Hey, what is happening now?" Sam asked, clutching on to Loxa. "You're now one of us by proxy: accepted as part of our clan by extension. We now take the flight of induction to honor that. Hold on and enjoy the flight," Loxa replied, mirth in his tone. The wyverns all tore through the night sky, and Sam had never felt such an exhilarating feeling in his life like it until then. He was upon the backs of great creatures that were thought to only have been of myth and legend until that very moment: what a revelation! Sam could feel their power by their sheer size while upon Loxa's back: the way their muscles moved with such fluidity and force, and the wind from such speeds of flight. To know that Sam had such powerful allies in his corner reassured him, for Rodrigo was making new shifters, and to what end of limits, Sam had no clue. As the clouds whooshed by in a blur below him, his thoughts briefly went to Sigma Pi, Fred, Sara, Ed, and his family, the idea of any harm coming to them by Rodrigo completely unacceptable.

"Sam," Loxa said, pulling the young man out of his thoughts in the sky, "We will head to Mount Elbert after this and begin planning what we can to aid in finding Rodrigo."

"Sounds like a plan to me," Sam replied, ready to work towards stopping the leopard king.

CHAPTER 9

ACROSS GREAT DISTANCES

The next day, Sam called Diego to fill the young kickboxer in on what was happening, after telling Sigma Pi of all that was to happen. Diego was mesmerized to hear that Sam was flying on the back of wyverns, but after his essence training at their initial meeting, Diego held little in cynical regard when it came to anything with the power or lore of shifters. Sam communicated the plans the wyverns had made with him the night before, upon the mountain where Illixus rested. The plan was to have most of the wyverns seek out any other members they could, while Sam and Loxa went to find Rodrigo. If the duo could strike first and hunt down his whereabouts, the potential for all future shifters could be dealt with.

"I see," Diego confirmed, listening to Sam explain all over the phone.

"You could use my help. If there's going to be numbers, you're going to want help."

"I initially didn't want to bring others for the fear of endangering them, but as a fellow essence user, I could certainly use your help. Not to mention, the prowess of Mexico's top ranked fighter going for his first world title? By all means!" Sam jested back, prompting a laugh from Diego.

"When do you plan on making the move? Do you know where Rodrigo is?"

"Not yet. Loxa and a few of the other wyverns are currently searching for any traces of him. While not as sensitive to essences as us, they can still pick up mild detections."

"Ah. Well then, keep me updated all that you learn. Once he's found, I say we take the fight to him."

"Yeah man. Until then, I'll talk to you later." Sam hung up the phone and got up from the recliner in his dorm living room. As he made his way to the door, a strange sensation of being watched came over him. Looking around, Sam tapped into his heightened senses to discern who or what may be in the area.

"Okay, if you're there, come out," Sam spoke into the empty dorm. "…w-wait…can you…actually sense me?" a female's voice

he had never heard before replied. "I can hear you in my head,"
Sam replied, his caution and nerves now on edge. "Who are you?"
"Oh wow…I actually contacted one," the voice replied, an uneasy
tone taking over her as Hanska appeared next to Sam. "Hi there,
I'm Fiona. I have special abilities that let me contact others across
great distances. I know it sounds silly, but I guess I reached you."
"Sam, she may be the user of an essence. I believe she's one of the
two final users we haven't met yet, granted that we know little
about the new ones of yet," Hanska added quietly, drawing a
concerned look from Sam.
"What business do you have with me?" Sam asked, not letting his
guard down. Deciding to probe without revealing too much, he
added, "Are you a psychic or something?"
"Not quite. I have…special abilities granted to me with a special
item, that lets me speak to others over long distances. I'm looking
for a particular group of people that can use things called
essences…in which…ah, this sounds so crazy even over the
phone! Who would believe this stuff?!" Fiona replied on the other
end of the mental line, growing exasperated. Sam could hear
genuine innocence in her voice, and didn't pick up any feeling
that she was working against him in any way, but he remained
vigilant regardless. The mention of essences alone had let him
know that he indeed was speaking with another user, one that
wasn't quite sure if he was or not.
"I know about them, yes. That still doesn't explain why you're
reaching out to me. What is your purpose?"
"I've been looking for other users like me," Fiona started, keeping
some form of guard up that finally went away when Sam
remained silent. "I'm looking for others like me, and I'm using a
focus called a spirit stone, to communicate to other potential users
across a distance. However, I think I got the wrong person, which
I completely apologize for."
"She's really candid. At least she's honest," Sam said to Hanska,
who had a look of interest on his stoic face.
"Ask about the spirit stone," he told Sam.
"What is this spirit stone you speak of Fiona? I'm willing to listen
to you for now. You sound interesting," Sam spoke, taking
command of the situation, and putting Fiona on the backfoot, yet
calming her down at the same time. "Oh, well in that case, only if

you're willing to hear something that will seem bizarre to normal people. It's a stone that comes from an ancient tribe that could shift into leopards from South America. I didn't believe it at first, but it has indeed worked for me, as I'm talking to you now."

"Sounds interesting. Can you read my thoughts?"

"I cannot. I can only speak with you over this connection."

Sam, getting more and more information that he wanted, kept going with his questions. "What powers do you exactly have?"

"I have an essence in me that lets me act as a medium with spirits. With it, I can also reach out to other souls and essence users. The spirit stone has let me contact you over a vast distance as such."

"Do you know how far the reach is from you? Sounds very impressive."

"I can't tell the distance from here, but it seems like you're a good measure away, from the feeling of it."

"It's certainly an interesting ability you have, Fiona," Sam stated, getting more of a feel of Fiona. She had no hostile intent in her tone, nor did it seem like she was out to cause Sam any harm. Still, with Rodrigo loose, he didn't put much past him and kept his caution up. "I have to go handle some business, Fiona. However, you seem like a nice person. A word of warning to you: watch out for certain people. They will see you use your abilities for the worse if they get the chance."

"Really?" Fiona asked, puzzled by such a comment. "Well then, I'll keep my eye out to make sure they wouldn't. So sorry to bother you!" The connection disappeared as Sam turned to face a troubled-looking Hanska. "What's the matter?" Sam asked, not used to seeing Hanska as anything less than stoic and composed. "She said…medium…as an essence user. She may very well have the druid medium essence. Which means…" Hanska began, trailing off.

"Which means what?"

Hanska crossed his arms and looked out of the window, his stare gazing off into the distance, then said, "She has the essence of my former beloved's soul." Fiona sighed, and took some time to clear her head of the fog that built up when she used the spirit stone, coupled with practicing her incomplete form of astral projection. As she did, a man in a purple suit and black fedora placed a gentle hand on her shoulder.

"Feeling okay?" he gently said.

"I'm fine, Mr. Viejas," Fiona replied, taking a sip of water from off the desk in front of her. "I'll get to trying again and finding more of the users. I didn't expect to find someone that wasn't."

"You did just fine," Mr. Viejas assured her. "I think I have enough information to make that work. When you feel ready, try and reach out again." Fiona nodded as Mr. Viejas calmly left the room and headed downstairs to leave the cabin. Outside, the weather was clear and chilly: both things Mr. Viejas loved.

"You're not as elusive or wise as you think you are, Sam. But have no worries, for you will be tested. I will personally see to it that you are assessed before we begin our final move," Mr. Viejas said to himself, walking to the black car parked outside. Getting in, he fired up the ignition and pulled out onto the black road near the cabin. "It's a shame, for you are such a brilliant kid. Alas, there's much work to be done, and it will soon come time for you to decide if you will aid us or impede us. Until then, make sure you prepare. The inevitable will come for you."

****

"She WHAT?!" Sam exclaimed, utterly shocked by the revelation.

"That woman has the druid medium essence. The very essence that was made with Marcela's spirit," Hanska replied.

"I didn't know she was sacrificed for that! Why didn't you tell me sooner?" Sam asked.

"It's…sensitive history for me. I was more focused on making sure you were improving to be able to stand up to Rodrigo. The only solace? The essence went to her sister Sarita. If things haven't changed since that, then Sarita is still the essence of the druid medium."

"Well then, we may end up having to meet up with Fiona yet. And still! That's horrible that happened! All I want to do now is take on Rodrigo even more!"

"In due time. Let us not jump the gun into any action as such." Hanska cautioned.

"Very true. What's our next move? "asked Sam.

"We may want to lay low. I have no doubt that Rodrigo may be building up and beginning to press his search harder for you."

The phone began ringing, and Sam, his nerves once again on edge, picked up.

"Hello?" he asked.

"Mr. Cruz, it's been a while! How are you?" the voice replied, soft, lilting, and kind.

"Who is this?"

"It's Mr. Viejas, of course. We met last year after your debacle with Bradley."

"And how did you get my number, asshole?"

"Those yellow pages books can be quite revealing, after all. Did you not think I remembered your address after taking the time to visit you?" Sam's blood went cold and realized that Mr. Viejas had known all along, and had simply taken no action against him the whole time.

"Don't tell me you're coming back to pay me a visit," Sam spat, his anger rising.

"That I am!" Mr. Viejas teased in a horrifying lighthearted tone. "Now, I am not Rodrigo, and don't seek to hurt you. I simply want to test your mettle, is all."

"Test me? You're already testing me!"

"That much is evident. But I want to test you in person. Assess, if you will. It will be one week until I show up. You have that much time to prepare by then."

"Prepare for what, exactly?"

"If I told you, you wouldn't truly prepare, now would you? Just more so the idea of preparation in one field, when you should be ready for anything." Sam wasn't impressed by the semantics that Mr. Viejas was giving him, but he also could understand the sentiment behind it, as a veiled meaning to prepare for beyond one field.

"I follow. One week, huh? Who's not to say you'd show up before then? Why should I trust you?"

"I give you my word. When you have my word, I absolutely refuse to break it. This much you can trust." Sam angrily gritted his teeth and felt his body tense up at the situation Mr. Viejas spoke of. On one hand, Sam felt pinned down by the situation, caught in what seemed to be a no-win scenario, with Mr. Viejas calling all the shots. Yet, Mr. Viejas had been honest in his nebulousness, the few times they had indeed interacted. "I need

more proof than your word of what you will do. Show me
something you are about now, and I'll be more inclined to believe
you."

"This is fair, Mr. Cruz," Mr. Viejas said on the other side of the
line, his voice calm and almost cheerful. It suddenly twisted into a
low whisper as he snapped, "I am the shadow master essence
user." Sam's jaw dropped, the revelation setting in as something
that he felt he somehow knew, but couldn't quite confirm until
now. The way Mr. Viejas spoke was both as an eager enemy and a
warm friend all at the same time, which only further confused
Sam from within.

"So, it's true, then? You're the other user?" Sam asked, trying to
regain some footing in their exchange. "Why yes I am. And the
person who called you is an associate of mine who has the other, if
I'm going to continue being honest with you. Don't worry, she has
no ill intentions to you or your friends. She's actually quite
friendly." Sam took another moment to process more of the
information revealed. Mr. Viejas had not only revealed himself,
but also confirmed that Fiona was one of the essence users. His
blatant show of honesty had Sam rattled, wondering just how
much Mr. Viejas was capable of.

"Sam?" Mr. Viejas added, stirring him from his thoughts, "I take it
that this will suffice as a show of my honor to you?"

"It will, I suppose. Hypothetically asking, if I were to not be here
around the week you wish to arrive, what would you do then?"

"Hmm…well, if that were indeed to happen, I would simply
proceed with other measures. You do have friends that live here if
I recall. But I know you, Sam. I know you enough to know that
you too are a man of principles, of a code of honor of your own,
and that you would never allow that to happen. You would never
be able to live with yourself if you did."

"How do you know so much about me, Mr. Viejas?" Sam asked
with more confidence, genuinely curious as to how Rodrigo's
right-hand man knew so much from such little interaction.

"Before I ever had an essence, I was a professional blackjack
player. I am but a man who genuinely enjoys the nature of
humans, how they think, how they behave. I suppose you could
almost call me a mentalist, except that I have a flair and panache
for a bit of showmanship and charisma in my dealings! In my

time, I've met many and shook hands with even more. Countless people, each with different traits that eventually began to recur in one another. You see, people are not so different as they believe themselves to be."

"I see. Well then, I suppose that's enough for now," Sam finished, taking control of the situation, ending the conversation after gleaning some insight back on Mr. Viejas.

"I suppose I'll see you here next week."

"Sounds good, Mr. Cruz. I look forward to meeting again." Hanging up the phone, Sam started pacing around the living room, deciding on what his next move would be.

"Hanska," Sam asked after a moment of pondering in silence.

"Yes?" the iron spiritualist replied.

"Should I send my friends away from the area on the day that Mr. Viejas arrives? I've got a gut feeling he won't be coming alone."

"Sam, your fraternity may be the edge you need to stand against whatever may happen in the coming days. I understand your caution in the matter, but do you wish to deal with Mr. Viejas alone, especially when he may bring others?"

"You're right. I'll inform everyone of what's going on and plan something from there. I need to call Diego as well, now that something is underway. Let's just hope Mr. Viejas is indeed a man of his word."

CHAPTER 10

MR. VIEJA'S TEST

A week passed from the call, and the sun began to set in the
Colorado mountains, casting long shadows across the land from
it. Sam stood with the Sigma Pi members in an open grassy area, a
safe distance from his dorm. Fred was with Hailey, Ed, and Sara at
the DuMont's, making sure to help protect them should trouble
find the house. Donte stepped up next to Sam and asked, "Well
then, once they're here, what do we do?"
"Hang back for now. Do not let Mr. Viejas know you have combat
capability. I don't trust him beyond saying he'd be here. He's
sharp. Extremely sharp. If he figures out that you're another
capable combatant, things could get nasty," Sam replied.
"Diego is on his way, but his flight seemed to be late from when
we last spoke." As soon as he said those very words, a handful of
cars appeared in the distance. Black ones, each reflecting the
evening glow of the sunset into foreboding beacons that were
approaching the area. The Sigma Pi members all stood at the
ready, watching in tense silence, save for the sounds of engines
and tires on the rocky gravel. Five vehicles in total all pulled up
and cut the engines before getting out. A slew of various young
women and men, all alike in age with the Sigma Pi, got out of their
cars. They were all wearing suits and blazer-skirt outfits, matching
one another. Finally, the last car's driver got out and revealed a
hulking person of a man. This member had no suit on, but regular
gray sweatpants and a black hoodie. He stood a head taller than
Sam and was well over his size. Despite Sam's own added
musculature from a year's time of training, it paled in physical
comparison at first glance to the other young man's burly size. A
man in a dark crimson suit, with a neatly trimmed mustache and
bowler stepped out of the passenger side, with a cane in hand.
Sam knew immediately who it was.
"Ah, Mr. Cruz, it is good to see you again!" Mr. Viejas chimed
jovially as he walked forward to greet Sam. He held his hand out,
offering a handshake. Sam just eyed him cautiously.
"Now now, there is no need to be so wary of a greeting. I told you
I would show up and take no action until we begin. I am a man of

my word." Sam decided to bite at the bait, seeing what his reaction would be and clasped hands. Mr. Viejas had a warm and surprisingly firm handshake for someone so wiry as he.

"See? No hostile intent here. I would sooner get rid of my right hand than break my word. Now then, we do have some business to attend to, and I have every intent on keeping my word in testing you."

"Yes, your vaunted test you've talked of. Get to it," Sam replied curtly, in no mood for Mr. Viejas's mirth.

"To the point, I see. Very well. Here's how it shall go," Mr. Viejas began explaining, swishing his right hand around while putting his left behind his back. "I will begin by having a test of spirit against you. As another essence user, I want to see just how capable you are. We will begin with essence manifestation and have a duel. Once we conclude that, we'll move on to a physical hand to hand match. You will fight Lars here for the second part." Mr. Viejas waved his hand to the large young man, whose face showed nothing but malicious intent leaking from his piercing green eyes, his short blond cropped hair only adding to his imposing figure.

"If you can manage and pass both, I will leave you with only my phone number if you need to contact me and nothing else. However, if you fail either one of them, then your friends will become hostages for our business firm." The Sigma Pi group all turned to look at Mr. Viejas with incredulity, almost disgusted with his gumption.

"The hell you will, old ass goon," Donte barked, his temper starting to rise.

"How you feel on the matter is irrelevant, good sir," Mr. Viejas calmly replied to him. "I have equal numbers with far more capability on my side. If Sam passes both tests, you needn't worry anyways."

"I don't understand," Sam interjected, drawing Mr. Viejas's attention to him. "You'd come out all this way just to simply test me, let alone leave a phone number if I win? What in the hell is that?"

"You almost sound disappointed, Mr. Cruz."

"I mean why would you make a trip all the way here just to waste your time if I kick both of your asses?"

Mr. Viejas grinned, enjoying Sam's rising bravado. "I'm here under orders to assess where you are is all. Being well in business with nothing but time and money, I have nothing better to do except what I must."

"With Rodrigo, I'd imagine."

"Well, in business with him? Yes. Directly his subordinate? Not so much. He is a partner of mine, but I by no means follow his orders. All these young men and women are a different story, but they currently answer to me."

"You mean you're willingly taking his side?" Sam exclaimed, baffled that anyone knowing what Rodrigo was about would do such a thing. "I am simply working as a partner of his. Nothing more, and nothing less. My own goals are not for you to know currently. Rodrigo did send me here to assess where you're at, yes. However, whereas he is more than okay with having you killed, I am not."

"You mean that if he were here, he'd just try to kill us all?"

"Oh yes. Rodrigo sees you as an impediment. He wants nothing more than to do away with you. I however don't want to see such a great young man with such potential go so quickly. I was the one that talked him down from going to take your life into simply coming here to assess you."

"I should be so lucky," Sam sarcastically snapped at him. Mr. Viejas shot him a serious look, the first Sam had ever seen from him and it put him back a step. "Sam, trust me when I say that there is more going on than just Rodrigo going for his own things. There are far more rivers flowing in motion than you can see right now. I'm doing you a favor by making sure you stay alive. How you perceive me is your own prerogative. I'm simply here to achieve a goal and purpose."

"Are you saying that I should trust you, despite being on Rodrigo's side?" Sam inquired.

"Interpret all of this as you will," Mr. Viejas cryptically replied. "I don't have to be your enemy. I am simply playing the part I need to."

"The part you need to, huh? Very well. Let's get this show on the road."

Mr. Viejas nodded and brought out a black shadow wreathed essence in front of him. "Very well, as you wish. Do not disappoint, Mr. Cruz." Sam brought forth Hanska at the ready, and was prepared to take on another essence user from the amount of practice he'd put in. Hanska rushed forth and swung at the shadow essence in front of him. The black figure almost dissipated, leaving wisps of darkness in its trail and shifted to the side. The iron spiritualist, having learned about the shadow master long ago, knew it wasn't a particularly strong being and relied more on tricks and craftiness to win. Sam was also aware of this and had Hanska only half-commit to attacking, more so as to observe the reactions and catch Mr. Viejas slipping. Another series of blows were thrown, and the shadow master would almost shift effortlessly in between blows, making circling movements. A second figure appeared behind Hanska, which was one of the tricks he had anticipated, and he drove a fist through the apparition immediately. The other essence moved forward to push an attack and was met with three solid blows, each one seemed to rattle Mr. Viejas a bit. This was the opening Sam wanted. Hanska took the initiative in delivering a constant stream of feints and foot shifts to lead to hits in mistimed evasions: the footwork drills from Diego certainly came in handy at this moment, and it was impressive that Mr. Viejas hadn't dropped his summoned essence yet. Another double of the shadow essence came out and Hanska was quick to dodge it when it tried to flank him from behind. A spinning back fist caught it in the head and dispersed it, which in turn slowed the main one up. Hanska then started delivering punches with much more power behind them, which all took but three of them to stagger Mr. Viejas. A final overhand right knocked the shadow off its feet, disappearing in a puff of smoke as Mr. Viejas dropped to one knee, shaking off the dizziness and pain. "Hurts, doesn't it? All of what one would feel in physical combat, still inflicted by mental and spiritual means?" Sam asked with crossed arms, having Hanska return to him. Mr. Viejas let out a chuckle in between breaths and slowly stood up. "Mr. Cruz, well done!" he complimented him. "You have far more skill in using your essence than I thought, as well as deadly intent when you fight. That is truly commendable. Now then, take a few minutes to get yourself ready to fight Lars here. This will be the second and final part. If you can defeat him, you're free to go as promised. Say, I'll even up my own ante: for defeating me: If you win against Lars, I'll pay your entire tuition for school off as well. More incentive to perform, yes?" Sam stared back, puzzled at the fact that Mr. Viejas was making deals again. "What's the catch?" "No catch. Same as before if you lose. I simply want to see you perform at your best against Lars. Incentive drives people to greater heights, after all."

"Very well," Sam replied, as Mr. Viejas walked over to him, and offered another hand forth. Taking his hand, the two shook on the deal before Mr. Viejas slightly wobbled back to the group, on his side where the cars were.

"Now then, I honestly believed the real challenge would have been me, so you may have an easier time with this one," Mr. Viejas said. "But then again, Lars is no pushover. He has a background in judo and karate."

"I'll take him on regardless," Sam quipped as the large young man that was Lars approached Sam. Sam put his guard up, and slowly moved forward to the lumbering Lars before him. "Very well, begin your bout!" Mr. Viejas exclaimed. Lars stepped forward with his guard up and steadily approached Sam. Sam waited until Lars was within range and took a leading jab at him, getting a gauge of distance and reach between them. Once Sam felt a light brushing of contact between them, he began to move more on the balls of his feet, remembering some of what Diego taught him during his time in Mexico. Lars moved in, sensing an opportunity to strike, and lunged deeply forward with a powerful right straight, one Sam was able to slip. He weaved in some and countered with a quick uppercut to Lars's midsection. If Lars was affected by the blow, he didn't show it, and Sam punching him felt like hitting a wall. Shuffling out of striking range, Sam began to plan his next move, when Lars moved in for another attack. Sam's reflexes had been heightened, due in part to training and the leopard within enhancing his reflexes. A series of lefts and rights came from Lars which Sam covered up to block, and stung back with a series of jabs. Lars doubled up on his advancing and threw another strong right, which Sam was getting used to seeing. Sam stepped back and threw a low kick to Lars's left leg and caught him on the quad, which seemed to have some effect. Sam knew he wouldn't win in an outright brawl with Lars, given his size, so he decided to play the long game and wear him down slowly. On and on Lars pressed, becoming more aggressive, and Sam kept on responding more and more with dodging, maintaining distance, and throwing strikes where he could. The Sigma Pi members continued to cheer Sam on, getting more riled up with time as Sam was gradually piling on the punishment, bit by bit.

"You're quick," Lars spoke in a deep voice. "Why don't you try and keep up with this?" Lars charged forth, and as Sam primed himself to deliver another counter, Lars suddenly shifted into a massive leopard form which completely threw Sam off. A missile of fur and muscle slammed into his chest, knocking him off his feet and on his back, driving the wind from his lungs. Sam quickly rolled to his side and propped himself up back to his feet, catching his breath, with Lars already back in his human form and drawing down upon him. On instinct, Sam moved to block one of Lars's blows and barely did so, only to get snatched up by the collar. Lars hoisted Sam into the air and drove a harsh fist into his ribs, a shock of pain rippling through Sam as he gasped for air. Another thunderous blow caught him in the jaw and Sam's vision started to go black around the edges. He had never been hit this hard in his life, Sam thought, and tried to desperately fight back from the fringes of his consciousness. He felt his fist hit something and suddenly felt weightless for a moment, as he felt his feet make contact on the ground. The black edges slowly ebbing from his sight, Sam staggered to keep his balance and saw that one of his punches made contact with Lars, with a stream of blood coming down from the side of his right brow. A murderous look was now painted on the behemoth of a young man's face, and Sam covered up again to regain his posture. Lars took his arms and wrenched his guard open with relative ease, leaving Sam unable to swing back with any punches. Lars moved in closely, reared his head back, let out a deep roar, then drove his head forward onto Sam's. The black edges were back, and quickly swallowed up Sam's vision as he felt his body go limp and fall into the darkness. Stirring briefly on the ground, Sam could hear various voices and saw feet shuffling about, His only guess being that the area was now a free for all. Finally, Sam felt himself fully fade into the black that eclipsed his sight, his body completely weightless.

CHAPTER 11

DEFEAT AND REVENGE

Sam was on a sunny beach with Sara, Fred, and Hailey, enjoying the crashes of the waves on the shore. He remembered the beach well: it was back home in Florida, where all seemed right with the world. "Sam, let's grab some drinks!" Sara exclaimed, pointing to one of the mobile drink trucks that would stop by. "I thought we were in Colorado," Sam thought to himself, but wondered if maybe they were indeed back home. The last few days were a blank to him, but he knew he was happy being back in Florida. The world's problems seemed so far out of reach for Sam. Everything was peaceful, warm, and sunny, which never led to a bad day in his eyes. As Sam walked with Sara to get a couple of cocktails, he asked her, "When did we visit Florida again?"

"We're back for vacation!" Sara replied. "The semester is done, so we returned here to enjoy time away, remember?"

"I suppose I don't," Sam sheepishly said, scratching the back of his head and wondering why there was a blank over the last couple of days. Sam was trying to recall details through a fog in his mind, as if something significant had occurred across that time span. The gnawing feeling of something important keep plaguing his mind, but he couldn't figure out what it was. Meanwhile, Fred and Hailey were happily playing on the shore, while Sara ordered them two screwdrivers.

"Sam, you seem to have something on your mind. Is everything okay?" Sara asked. "I…I feel like there's something important back in Colorado I have to handle…but I don't remember what," Sam replied, looking on at the ocean as he took a sip from his glass.

"Sam. We're here on vacation. We're not here to think about Colorado right now. All is fine, all is well is in the world, sweetie. You're still carrying Keystone here. Why don't we go relax near the water? That seems to usually help."

"Yeah, I suppose you're right," Sam replied, taking another sip of his drink as the two went to a blanket they had set out there. The two of them sat there, gazing upon the water, and Sam was able to feel somewhat more at ease. The crashing of the waves was a relaxing sight and sound to the young man, one that did indeed help relieve any worries or stress. The feeling of something off sat further back in his mind, as he saw a stray cat walk along the shore. "Aw look, little guy must live around here!" Sam said as he watched the animal trot along the shoreline. It had exotic features in its fur: a nice shade of tan and orange, with ringed spots. The cat moved along and turned to head in the direction where Sara and Sam sat. "Aw look, I think it's heading this way!" Sara exclaimed. The cat did indeed make a straight line for the couple, until it was no more than five feet away or so and sat down in front of them. "Why hello there!" Sam chimed at the cat. "Do you want something to eat?"

"No, but I'm sure they do," the cat suddenly replied, startling Sara and Sam.

"They? Who is they?" Sam asked, the worry starting to quickly return to his head. The cat motioned and pointed with its tail to the shoreline and replied, "Them." Coming from the waves, a slew of leopards all broke through the waves and slowly sauntered towards the shoreline, a deadly calm of poise and intent in their eyes. Sam popped up to his feet, on his guard while Fred and Hailey joined up with him, Fred getting ready to stand his ground with Sam. The small cat began to shift into a humanoid form, one of that of a hulking, grotesque shape of something between an abnormally large human, ape, and cat. The sight of it made Sam's stomach drop, fear and horror starting to set in, as the leopards all gathered around, waiting to see what the feline-turned monster would do.

"Turn away from your path. You cannot hope to win against the others!" the monster growled in a deep, guttural voice that rattled Sam's nerves. The fighting instinct from within surfaced in a rush of adrenaline and blood, as he prepared to fight against what seemed to be a hopeless situation.

"And just let you win? If I'm going to go down, I'm not going without a fight!" Sam cried in a desperate rage as he turned into his own leopard form. He watched as the monster lumbered to him, hearing Sara and Hailey distantly scream in the background as he slid with great agility under its leg, slashing at a thigh and drawing blood. As Sam pounced up and landed on its back, prompting a horrifying roar, he saw the other leopards around all sprint in slow motion for him and the hulking creature. His last sight were teeth and claws all bared, sailing through the air to get him, followed by a converging of fur and bodies, turning everything black. Sam was floating through the silent darkness, the beach, his loved ones, all gone except him. An isolated, lonely feeling of panic began to take him over. A voice barked through the darkness, snapping his attention to it, crying out, "WAKE UP!!!" Sam felt the darkness lift from the voice, and give way to a blinding white light that blurred his vision. Sam sat up with a jolt and felt a rush of pain shoot from his head and down his body. Breathing hard and looking around confused, Sam's senses were catching up to him as he took stock of where he was. He was back in his dorm, in his bed, surrounded by Sara, Diego, Hailey, and Fred.

"Where…what happened?" Sam asked, his breathing returning to a somewhat normal cadence." Looking out of his window, he saw that it was nighttime.

"Where's Mr. Viejas, and the others? The Sigma Pi members?"

"They were taken hostage by the others," Fred somberly replied, a look of worry on his face. "You were on the ground when Diego found you and brought you inside."

"…that means I failed the others," Sam replied glumly, looking to one of the walls.

"Sam, I'm just glad you're okay," Sara softly said, sitting next to him on the bed and gently putting a hand to his chin.

"But the others are gone! I failed them because I lost!" Sam exclaimed, feeling desperation and anger well up in him again. "What do we do now?"

"I may be able to help with that," a female's voice spoke as a dark-skinned woman with curly long blond hair walked in, her hazel eyes meeting his.

"Your voice sounds familiar," Sam said, trying to put a finger on where he heard speak before. "I'm Fiona, the druid medium essence user," Fiona replied, with Sam only showing surprise.

"So, you're the one that contacted me. How did you find this place?" Sam asked.

"I followed Mr. Viejas here since I have a relic called the spirit stone. He told me about the test he had in mind for you, and I

realized that I may have a chance to meet the iron spiritualist. Not only that, but the blood beast is here too!"
"You work for Mr. Viejas?" Sam growled, sitting up in anger. "YOU'RE the one that helped lead him here?!"
"No!!! All I did is come here of my own accord!!! I had no want of any of this happening, nor knowing what Mr. Viejas would do!" Fiona shrieked and cowered back in fear as Sam swung his legs off the bed and got to his feet. He started advancing for Fiona before Diego stepped in between them. "Sam!" Diego sternly said, containing Sam in a bear hug, "I already spoke with her. She genuinely didn't know any of this was going on until now!"
"OUR FRIENDS ARE GONE BECAUSE OF MR. VIEJAS! BECAUSE OF YOU!" Sam bellowed in anger, while Fiona backed into the wall with her hands up. "I'm sorry for what they did!" Fiona whimpered. "I promise I had no knowing of what would happen!"
"Then prove it!" Sam roared, Diego holding him back even tighter. Hanska appeared and walked to the terrified Fiona, hoping to diffuse the rising situation.
"Child, can you prove to me you are innocent of knowing of all of this?" he gently said,
"She indeed can," the female essence she had replied, also making an appearance.
Now it was Hanska's turn to express shock, as he stopped in his tracks while the woman looked at him and explained, "I've been with her this entire time, and she's had no knowledge. Mr. Viejas has had her in the dark until now. You know honesty as well as I do when you see it, Hanska."
"S…Sarita? Is that really you?" Hanska choked out. Sarita nodded with a small smile and replied, "It is, indeed. It has been a while, hasn't it?" Hanska turned to face Sam, then confidently spoke,
"Fiona is not guilty of such heinous plans." Sam felt himself calm down a bit upon seeing her essence come out, and asked Sarita, "Is this true? Are you covering for her?"
"I am not, young man," Sarita replied.
"She is as innocent as you are. If you wish, let me show you."
"Show me," Sam demanded, not quite satisfied. Sarita walked to Sam and entered his body, where Sam felt a cold chill and another presence with him. A rush of thoughts suddenly appeared in his

mind, thoughts that were memories: and they were not his own, but Fiona's. The scene in Sam's mind started with meeting Mr. Viejas and Rodrigo in person, shaking hands and learning that the work to be done would be to meet with people around the world, and claim real estate on places. A blur forward and the scene morphed into Fiona meeting various people in a hastened pace of speed, going about meeting with points of contacts, laying groundwork for Mr. Viejas and the places he sent her. Another blur rushed past Sam in a surreal manner, and he saw the ghastly apparition of a samurai attacking, with Fiona holding him off in sheer fright and desperation. Soon after, one caught his attention as he listened to a visibly saddened Mr. Viejas tell the tale of his old friends that were lost at sea. He went into detail of how he ultimately wanted to retire in Ireland, once the business he had begun with his partner was done. Sam noticed genuine desire at the words he said, and the conversation stuck with him in his thoughts. From the memories Sam experienced as they kept shifting, he learned that Fiona was indeed kept in the dark, and ignorant of events leading to the current time. The scenes would continue to increase in speed until it all melded together in Sam's head, and concluded with a flash of light as he returned to his dorm room.

"Well Sam, did you get the answers you were looking for?" Sarita asked. Diego released Sam when he felt his body relax, and Sam slowly began walking to Fiona. Fiona was in tears by that point, and pressed up against the wall, scared of what Sam may do next. "I apologize for unloading on you like that," Sam gently said, his face now devoid of any of the anger from earlier.

"Mr. Viejas is involved with less than savory characters that have caused us trouble in the past, and has taken my friends even now. I couldn't be sure if you were in cahoots to that extent with him or not. I see now that you tell the truth." Fiona looked at him and sniffled, wiping the tears off her cheeks, she choked out, "No, I'm the one who should be sorry. Had I known that he was capable of such terrible things or wanted them to, I wouldn't have been so quick to work with him. And now…now your friends are kidnapped because of it!" Diego walked over to her and gently put a hand on her shoulder, then said, "Mija, it is okay. No one here is angry with you now. Our rage lies with Mr. Viejas, and

Rodrigo. They are our true enemies. Having you with us may just be the edge we need in figuring out how to get Sam's friends back." Fiona looked at Diego with a relieved face, touched by his show of compassion.

"He's right," Sam added, nodding his head. "Having three essence users together is far better than one or two. Plus, we have the fourth locked away in the seal."

"The Oro Luna, right?" Fiona asked.

"You know of it, then?"

"Yes. Sarita told me the history of the clan and some of their artifacts, like the seal and the spirit stone."

"It seems we've got more collective knowledge here than we originally thought we'd have," Diego interjected. "Perhaps we should all relax and take some time to acquaint ourselves better, before getting to a plan of action? That way, we'll all be on the same page before doing so."

"I like that idea very much," Sam replied. Turning to Fred and Sara, he asked, "I've got some food in the fridge, but it isn't enough to feed everyone. Should we go get some?"

"No worries, Sam," Fred replied. "I grabbed some cold ones earlier before heading to Ed's, and planned on ordering some pizzas. You just take it easy for now, man. You've had a rough day today." The group's faces all seemed to agree warmly with the idea of a pizza dinner as Sam said, "All right, pizza it is! Come on everyone, let's go to the living room and we'll plan from there!"

"Sam, it is incredible how quickly you recover as is. When food gets involved? Nothing stops you," Sara teased as the group moved to the living room.

CHAPTER 12

PLANNING THE COUNTERATTACK

"As of present, here is how things stand," Sam began with everyone sitting around in the living room, listening intently. "We have an unknown number of these new shifters. I'm not sure if they have the same essences as we do, especially since the original six are not split like they once were. Obviously, finding them will be the first task, which is already underway." Fiona looked to Sam and asked, "Already? How?" Sam held a thumbs up and responded, "I'll explain that part later. Let's just say…I know some valuable people to help with that."

"If you say they're on it, I trust you," Diego added. "What then?"

"Once we get a confirmed location, I think it's best that we get some information on numbers, and what we're working with. If the numbers are far too much, we need to make a rescue and run kind of deal the focus. Obviously, getting the Sigma Pi boys is number one regardless. However, if they don't have such numbers, we may just stand a chance on taking them down then and there."

"Sounds reasonable," Diego acquiesced. "If they have far greater numbers than anticipated, I suppose we'll retreat for the time being and regroup after?"

"Pretty much," Sam confirmed, nodding his head. Taking a sip of his beer, he continued, "If we can get any information on Rodrigo that we don't know yet, that will likely help us out as well. We're either fighting or pulling off a hit and run of sorts; either way, we can't just let our guys be captured." Turning to Fiona, Sam asked, "Fiona, does Mr. Viejas know you're here?"

"No. I intentionally kept my presence hidden from him since he seemed nebulous on what he was doing out here when we talked," Fiona explained. "He's usually incredibly open with me in terms of when he goes to do something, he just seemed adamant on not letting me in on what was going. Judging from his tone on the phone call however, I had a gut feeling that something was going to happen. That, and finding out from him that another essence user was confirmed here? I had to come see."

"It's good to have you with us, Fiona. We're going to need you with us in the days to come against Mr. Viejas and Rodrigo," Sam explained. "This is going to make things complicated with Mr. Viejas and my work, but no one should be kidnapped and held against their will," Fiona surmised. "I didn't even know there was another side to the whole operation they were doing! I just meet with people to establish relations for them, so they acquire real estate holdings for them."

"Acquiring locations around the world? Sounds like the old Jan Damis coming back into the modern day," Sam explained.

"I'm familiar with their history, thanks to Sarita," Fiona added. "Then it also stands to reason that there's a good chance they're slowly expanding operations, and making new users through unknown means. How? I'm not exactly sure, but after taking on Lars, Mr. Viejas wasn't bluffing on that part."

Diego took a bite of his pizza, swallowed, looked to Fiona and asked, "Can you tell us a bit about all he's capable of? The more we know, the better we can deal with him if we encounter him again?"

"Of course," Fiona replied. "Mr. Viejas has the shadow master essence, as we all know. He can form shadow copy illusions of himself. One replica copy illusion can give him extra eyes and ears in another location. As far as I know, he can't just send it away as far as he wants: there's limits to the distance, usually within fifty feet or so, give or take from what I've seen. His shadow ability also slightly alters his physical features with illusions, which only adds to the natural mysteriousness he already has. It's not physical strength that makes him dangerous, it's his charm, wit, charisma, guile, and tact."

"I can attest to that a bit myself," Sam agreed. "He could read me over the phone like a book when we spoke. If he's just that much of a natural, I can only imagine his essence amplifying that."

"Speaking of him: if he found you here before, it may be wise to switch to dorms," Fred interjected. "He has our address and number, we're effectively a target now."

"A good point. Let's get that rolling as soon as we can," Sam agreed. "Well then, sounds like have an immediate plan of action to put into play now, any other things to add that I may have missed?"

"While your contact looks for your friends' whereabouts, I can use the spirit stone to see if I can get wind of where the other new essence users are. Not only that, but I can also speak with Mr. Viejas on the go and keep his attention away from you. I know it sounds silly as a countermeasure, but he is immaculately sharp on details and small things as I've learned," Fiona explained.

"That will help us greatly," Diego concurred. "By the way, Sam and I would love to see you using the spirit stone. Perhaps it can give us the edge we need in stopping Rodrigo." Fiona smiled and replied, "I'd be happy to! On one condition though. Can you tell me about Rodrigo now? I spoke much with Sarita on who he was in the tribe, and I've really only seen him once without knowing who he actually is now."

"Rodrigo is many things, and none of them good," Sam began. "He took the former Sigma Pi head here under his wings, and tried to have him attack us while he reacclimated to the world. He doesn't seem to regard human life all that much, so not a far cry from who he was then. He's gone into hiding somewhere, as far as I know, so I couldn't tell you much beyond that."

"Maybe we'll just find out for ourselves when we see him again. I don't think he's going to be any different really, if he's still trying to do the same things he did, thousands of years ago," Diego said in a low voice, cracking his knuckles.

"A very true point," Sam agreed, crossing his arms. "Ultimately, stopping Rodrigo will be the final endgame here. Having the Oro Luna in our possession will help with sealing their numbers away, but we should learn more on how many can be sealed at a time." Hanska appeared next to Sam and added, "The Oro Luna at one point could seal dozens of souls at a time. If I had to guess, you'll only be able to seal all but a handful at a time now. Now, bear in mind, the seal was only meant to hold the original six. Because the essences were only fragmented across a whole mass of others, it was easy for the Oro Luna to seal away. Think of it as collecting fragments of six bigger pieces to a puzzle. Now? I'm not so sure. These new users have their own from sources unknown. I don't know if the seal can hold them all, and if it can, it may absorb them much slower."

"That helps to know," Sam acknowledged. "Then we'll have to try carefully. If we end up finding one or two alone and taking their essence, that will confirm if the Oro Luna can take on new essences. If not, what do we do from there?"

"Ultimately, taking Rodrigo's essence from him or taking his life will do it. When the jaguar king's soul was used to form Rodrigo's essence, he cursed him with either his essence leaving him by death or with the Jaguar Clan's sealing artifact which they made, which is the Oro Luna. Rodrigo would indeed have immortality otherwise, but these are the two ways to stop him."

"Wasn't he in the seal himself though, before he was released? Won't the seal just put his entire being away again?" Fred asked.

"There's a special method to sealing him off instead of the others," Hanska explained. "It requires all of the other essences to bind his own. Last time, he was sealed without the help of any of the others, which preserved him. It requires the essences of the shadow master, druid medium, iron spiritualist, war chief, and blood beast to do so. We will all need to be actively out when you begin sealing him, for we will battle his own essence and peel it away from his physical body. Once we do so, then we will all need to be sealed away. After that, Rodrigo will be merely mortal."

"Then it's settled. We either we seal his essence off or kill him," Sam affirmed aloud. "I'd rather not take life if I can avoid it personally, so I'm more for the sealing option. Thoughts, guys?"

"I have no want of murdering anyone, so killing is out of the question for my vote," Fiona inputted. Diego shrugged and explained, "I don't mind if he ends up dead. Whether he gets killed or sealed? That's his fault for ever doing this in the first place. Sure, sealing him away would be the more sensible thing. However, for someone that not only has tried to harm each of us here in some way, but has sacrificed people before in his time.... if he needs to be dealt with permanently that way, I'm not against it either."

"I suppose we're going for the sealing option first, then," Sam finished. "If that fails, then I understand we may have to go the more extreme route. Now, here's the next question: how do we get the war chief to help us when there's no host?"

"A new one will need to house the essence," Hanska calmly replied. "You will need to find a new host. The essence by itself cannot aid in sealing away Rodrigo."

"A new host? That adds some complications to things," Sam stated, thinking about the ramifications. "Wait, can't one of us with an essence take another?"

"No," Hanska replied, shaking his head. "Once someone has an essence, they cannot have another. The human body cannot hold two."

"That means we'd need to find someone who was willing to inherit the war chief," Fiona added. "I don't suppose anyone here would want an essence of the old Parduska Clan, right?" Sam asked, turning his focus to Fred and Sara. Sara shook her head, held her hands up and replied, "I have no want of anything to do with essences anymore, to be honest. I'm sick of the whole thing." Fred sighed and replied, "Having the abilities of leopard, what exactly does that all entail?" Diego looked to him and said, "You have another being within you that can help you understand how things work, to start. Your senses get an overhaul and become much sharper, as well. The world seems clearer through your eyes. Sounds are crisper. You can almost sense someone out of your line of sight without knowing they're even there. Your smelling picks up scents that would take you standing much closer to the source than usual. It's like living on an enhanced level. There's few things like it."

"It's that good, huh?" Fred responded after a moment of digesting the information. "And the shifting into a leopard?"

"Takes some getting used to at first, but it does make a difference when you have it," Fiona answered. "I'm still grasping the concepts to mastering the form better myself, but Sam and Diego would probably be better at it." Fred stroked his chin with thumb and forefinger, then looked at Sam and replied, "Well buddy, what do you have to say on it?"

"Diego and Fiona pretty much described it to the nines. And if you don't want it in you forever, don't worry about it: once we seal Rodrigo, the others will join in to seal him as well," Sam explained. "That is correct, right, Hanska?"

"Correct. The Oro Luna will seal it back up along with the others, once Rodrigo is dealt with. That is, if you are willing. It's still an adjustment, so do not take this lightly, Fred." Fred clenched his fist and staunchly spoke, "No, I think I should. I want to stand by my friend and fight alongside him. To think in a year, he went

from barely being able to defend himself, to being the one doing all the fighting. I can't watch Sam just continuously stick his neck out for us all. No way, not if I have a chance of helping. My family will be at risk if Rodrigo should ever succeed. The Sigma Pi guys need us. We need more essence users. I have too much to lose, and lots to…" Fred trailed off as he looked to Hailey with a flare of determination and softness in his eyes. "I have her to protect as well," Fred slowly said, his voice growing more mellow in tone. "Fred, whatever you choose to do, I will support you," Hailey gently replied, seeing the turbulent conflict he was having with potentially becoming the new war chief. "If that's what you truly wish to do, then we can make it happen," Sam added, his tone also softer. "Only if you genuinely want to do this. If you do, the three of us will help you and teach you everything we know."
"I would love that," Fred said as he got up off the couch. "Let's do this. If we're going to take Rodrigo down, I'm sure we're going to have a slew of essence users to battle through." Diego chuckled and responded, "Oh I hope we do. My fists crave blood." Sam added, "There's a guy named Lars that I fought, way bigger and stronger than the rest of them. He was certainly more than a challenge for me. Perhaps you'd like a shot at him."
"Oh, to deliver vengeance for a friend? I would love nothing more than that," Diego growled with a grin that bordered on malicious. Sam could feel his mere willpower starting to come to the surface, bringing a familiar pressure he had felt when he was sparring with him in Mexico." Fiona timidly interjected, "Please don't ever look at me like that. That's just scary." Diego was pulled from his thoughts on fighting Lars at the sound of Fiona's gentle tone, and his facial features relaxed as he turned his focus to her. "Ay, no mija! I wouldn't dare put my fury to you," Diego explained, his tone much more apologetic and lighthearted. Running a hand through his silky black hair, he added, "You've proven to be a worthy ally so far. If you're truly with us for the battle ahead, then I would give my life to protect you, or any of the people here. Any friend of Sam's is a friend of mine." Fiona blushed at his words as Sam said to the group, "Well then, I think we're all in agreement on what to do. The next step is getting Fred the war chief essence, then applying to switch dorms tomorrow. From there, we'll get to work on locating their headquarters or wherever they're at, rescue

the Sigma Pi guys, escape, and then consolidate to make one last push to stop Rodrigo. We only stay and fight if we absolutely have no choice. Getting the others is our top priority, then getting out so we don't risk any lives. Are there any questions on the plan?" "Just one. When do we begin?" Fred smirked as he clapped a hand on Sam's shoulder. Sam turned to face his childhood friend and replied with an equally brazen smile, "Right now."

CHAPTER 13

BUILDING AN ARMY

Within the week, a building hidden near a mountain was newly constructed, and sat tucked away amongst a cluster of trees in a forest. As the clouds passed over, the sun struggled to pierce through the gray skies, and in turn, gave way to the rising of fog in the area. Within the compound, dozens of young men and women all went about their day, doing various activities from simply enjoying banter, to training with one another in combat, hiking, and tactics. Several leopards ran by two men walking across the freshly cut grass, as they headed to a pavilion made of logs and stone that was recently constructed. The man in the hat said to the other, "Well now, this place has flourished rather nicely. Lots of new recruits, I can see. You've been busy." The other man in the suit replied, "Yes, we've been growing the ranks quite well. The prison idea truly has let us grow our numbers quickly. We're currently at forty members and rising."

"Quite the spectacle," the man in the hat mused. He secretly hid his disgust at the process of making new essence users, finding the practice and ritual of it barbaric and a waste of life. Sure, they had their disagreements on some practices, but this one resonated deeply within him.

"Mr. Viejas," the other man asked, "How did running into Sam go? What did you learn?" Mr. Viejas smiled and replied, "He's well, Rodrigo. He's certainly grown in his abilities. The way he fought against Lars was impressive. However, Lars is in a league of his own."

"No doubt," Rodrigo replied. "Of all the recruits I brought on, he had something different in him. He wasn't just another ordinary college student. No, he had drive and fire from within him. You see, when I found him, I learned his whole backstory when I asked why he would be good with the company as a bodyguard."

"And what is that I may ask?"

"He came from a rough neighborhood upbringing that twisted his drive and perception into something monstrous," Rodrigo began, his eyes lighting up. "Lars grew up in an abusive household where his father constantly beat him and his mother. He was often picked on for being small, and constantly in fights for it. Growing up, he didn't know much of comfort, because their family was constantly in poverty. Shame, squalor, hunger, you name it, he experienced it. Over time, this all began to compound into seething rage and contempt for humanity."

"I see," Mr. Viejas said, ascertaining that Rodrigo must have had a soft side for those with a propensity for psychopathy.

"What happened next?"

"He grew stronger by getting into sports and ended up growing into his own. He became a mighty force of nature and anger, fueled by desire to not fall into poverty again. When I offered him the chance to work as security with us, he jumped at it without fail. When I tested him, he passed with flying colors and ruthless tenacity. The pinnacle of muscle and focus, especially with his new essence. I'm not surprised Sam lost to him to be honest."

"Seeing his ability firsthand, I'm not either. I take it you're rewarding him handsomely for such devoted work to you, yes?" Mr. Viejas asked. Rodrigo smiled and replied, "With no reservation. He's certainly earned the spot as the top guy in our security group. I try not to have favorites, so I effectively made him my left-hand man, since you're already at my right."

"He seems quite well to do for the job," Mr. Viejas humored Rodrigo. "Speaking of personnel, how many do you plan to gain for our grand total?"

"The prison is quite low on death row inmates now, so the numbers will remain as they are for now. Forty should be quite enough for the time being. I know I said I wasn't going to reform the Jan Damis, and I stand by that. However, I do plan to use these forty here to start making their way into key positions of power, much like back in the past. And this time, no splitting essences needed."

"You're the one with the vision. I'm just here to help you realize them easier," Mr. Viejas said with a flourish of his hand. "All things of reality, we must impose our will upon to make happen. You do just that."

"Indeed. And once I get these young men and women to the positions they need to be in, it will leverage us to eventually start moving our aims to the world. No secret society, just all of us as one group moving forth. There will not be much to stop us."

"Unless you count the other two essence users. But what power do they have against all of us? Lars alone was enough to take Sam down. If he cannot be beaten there, what hope would they have?"

"You were right in going to see and assess his abilities," Rodrigo conceded. "He may yet be more useful to us alive than dead. I'm glad you convinced me to not have him killed outright."

"Yes. He's more useful to us alive," Mr. Viejas agreed, while holding his own thoughts in. Mr. Viejas genuinely liked Sam for the person he was, as well as being a potential key piece on the board to use later. While Mr. Viejas was happy to work with Rodrigo, questions on his ethics and methods began to drive a wedge between them. Mr. Viejas was no stranger to violence or death, but to resort to it so quickly and gleefully instead of talking first? He didn't care for it. How happily and eagerly Rodrigo used it, especially with the essence ritual, only made him even more distrusting. The two continued to walk the grounds of their new compound which they had acquired a few months back, with Mr. Viejas figuring out what he was to do with Rodrigo. The leopard king himself was slowly growing more detached from reality, from morals, from ethics. Mr. Viejas could justify initially working with him, but he had seen enough crazy people in his time to know that when morals and ethics went out the window, it would only be a matter of time until the same fate was to befall him. Was it too much to ask to just be a casino player, to earn easy money with his abilities, and live a nice life? Mr. Viejas knew that sometimes the world needed a violent push now and then against it, but Rodrigo was becoming more unstable in his eyes as time went on.

"Rodrigo, you know we could focus on the business for the time being, and build our position to make taking the other ones easier and less forceful," he began, trying to feel where Rodrigo would stand on that sentiment.

"We've focused plenty on it," Rodrigo replied, as if continuing to focus on it was heinous. "That's what I have you for. You handle the business; I handle bringing the new talent on to set us up for more power. The people there don't have much of a choice. It's just getting them into the natural pieces and accelerating their movement up. I'm starting with smaller companies for them to easily get into. From there, we devour any that stand in our way on the way up, and begin powering our way into bigger companies. After that, the political system. It would take most decades to get there, but for us? Maybe two years at best. Expansion and growth must happen, and we will do just that."

"This is the modern world, Rodrigo. There are far more technological advances that pose a risk in security. It will be much harder to get away with things like assaults and murders. I stress tact and subtlety because I do not want to see anything happen to our group. Better we move unhindered and save the violence as a last resort."

"I see your concerns, my friend. Now yes, I understand that back in the era of my tribe, things were different. And as such, we must move more gently in a modern world that sees less face to face war," Rodrigo explained, his face taking in all Mr. Viejas had told him. "That does not mean I will not hesitate to use force if needed, however. Violence is a tool, a means to an end if we need it to be. Never forget that. If Sam is as good as you say, he has room to grow yet. If he crosses my path, I will take him out if need be. I do not plan on leaving anything to chance. Arrogance is what had me sealed up centuries ago. I will not make that same mistake again."

"I understand," Mr. Viejas acquiesced, deciding not to push the envelope any further. He had made his point with Rodrigo and didn't want to further press the issue. He glanced over to the field where the recruits were practicing combat and saw Lars. The large security leader was taking on two other recruits, both rushing him with a series of blows. For such a large stature, Lars moved quickly and managed to avoid getting hit, before countering one with a sharp jab and a spinning back fist to the other. Both the other two combatants were knocked off their feet, stunned and dazed from such force. Mr. Viejas wondered just how much of a threat Lars would ultimately pose to Sam if they met again. By nightfall, Rodrigo was speaking to the forty students he had under him in the great dining hall. A spread of various foods was arranged in a ceremonious manner, with wine goblets and silver plates. The students listened on, eagerly tearing into their cuts of venison, roasted duck, baked potatoes, and more. "Now, I'm glad you are all here and enjoying your feast. Tonight, marks an incredibly important milestone for us," Rodrigo began, taking a sip from his favorite port red wine. "We have officially grown our numbers to where we can begin our real conquest. You see, working here has lined your pockets well." The students at the table all cheered their agreement with bright smiles and sidebar chats of approval. "We are going to begin our next phase of integrating with society and making it our own. I have a list of companies that not only await you to join their ranks, but from there, we will accelerate your position to eventually take over them. Each one of you will be assigned to the companies I have spoken to: some by individuals, some by groups. Within, you will work up to secure your places at the top levels. Once you do, we can begin moving into the political system. But for now, this is your focus and task. Whatever you learned in college? May it help you to the top. If it doesn't get rid of it. Our time at the top will begin. Thus, we have this feast tonight to commemorate your next grand move!" The tables roared with applause and cheers, the young men and women around, all excited to take on their new task. Mr. Viejas was in one of the offices while the feast was going on to make some calls on Rodrigo's behalf. One of the calls he started dialing to make was for Fiona. He held the receiver to his face and listened to the dial tone ring through to the proper channels.

"Hello?" Fiona's voice answered on the other end. "Fiona, how are you this evening?" Mr. Viejas asked, looking out the window to the moonlit grounds.

"Just got back from the grocery store, getting ready to cook dinner. How are things on your end?"

"Enjoying a wonderful night here at the new Leo Compound in the Washington nature out here."

"Oh, that's exciting! A new HQ finally up?" Fiona excitedly asked.

"You could say that. More so a branch for other fields of development for other members. They're currently celebrating a dinner in the hall."

"Well, why aren't you with them? Shouldn't you be celebrating alongside them? They'd love to have you in their company!" Fiona asked. Mr. Viejas chuckled pensively and replied, "I've already had my celebrating with them. Currently have some calls to make, so I'm in the office following up with other entities. I figured I'd check up on you." he said.

"All is well on this end. You sound tired, however. Is everything okay on your end? You're not the usual mysterious, exciting Mr. Viejas I've come to know."

"All is well, dear. I've been working myself a wee ragged of late, is all. Lots going on that demands my attention and efforts. Do I really sound that worn down?"

"It's noticeable. You can't push yourself so hard without rest. Why don't you get some sleep after a few more calls?"

"You're right, Fiona. I'll do that."

"Very good! I'll leave you to your calls. I will be on a small vacation for the time being, so I will keep you updated as I go. I'm going to start dinner. Get some rest now, okay?"

"I will. Enjoy your evening and vacation coming up." Mr. Viejas hung up the phone in the cradle, took a deep breath and gazed upon the moon. "I must be faltering a bit if Fiona can tell I'm off my game. I'm always on point: I need to get back to it," he mumbled to himself as he looked upon the beautiful moonlight outside. Sighing, he muttered to himself, "Sam, I hope you have the strength to save your friends. I cannot just release them as so."

CHAPTER 14

THE SPARK OF HOPE

Another week had gone by while Sam awaited his contacts regarding the status of Rodrigo's whereabouts. During that time, he and Diego were training Fred on how to better use the war chief's essence. Fiona had returned to Colorado to aid where she could on the knowledge of spirits and essence manifestation. Hanska and Sarita had also caught up within the time, overjoyed to have reunited once again in their current lifetime. Piero would eventually come around once Fred was linked closely enough with his essence. Until then, Fred had help from three mentors, with which he rapidly grew. Sam would teach about mental fortitude and the importance of the link with one's essence, and how a higher mental resilience meant a stronger link. Diego had the combat training covered, which Fred was eager to take to, and soon came to revere Diego for, regarding his skills. He had been in some fights in his time, but Diego was aiming to become a world champion in kickboxing for his country. The skill level was beyond what Fred was used to. Fiona would cover the spiritual side in making one more aware to one's own self and essence, by communication and projection. While Fiona had the lowest battle prowess of the others, her ability to manifest her essence was the best of them all. While not as mentally resilient as Sam, Fiona was the most spiritually capable, thanks in part to her paranormal sensitivity and druid medium training. Fred was greatly enjoying his newfound abilities: the heightened senses, the added stamina, the leopard form, and increased awareness. Hailey had also taken notice of the changes, and said that he had a wilder presence about him than before. Sara had informed Ed about the situation at hand, and he offered up any books or items that would aid in helping the group for their coming confrontation with Rodrigo. Later in the evening, the lot of them went to SRV for dinner, where they were in much better spirits. "Haven't come here in a while, feels good to be back," Sam said, taking a sip from his soda. "We've been so caught up in this essence fiasco that we haven't taken much time to just enjoy life."

"I know what you mean," Fred added, swallowing a bite of his burger. "This place was always hopping with the Sigma Pi guys. One more reason to bring them home safely, so we can get this place loud and lively again."

"I would like to meet these guys myself when we finally rescue them," Diego added. An older man with silver hair and a peppered gray beard walked up to the table and said, "You guys been talking about that folklore of that leopard tribe of late. Couldn't help but hear. What's brought such an interest about it?"

"Oh, John! Hello there, care to have a seat with us?" Sara said to the owner as Fred, Hailey, and Sam looked on in recognition. "Ah, no thank you, just checking in on y'all."

"We've been talking plenty on the lore of it because it's true," Sam answered. John crossed his arms and replied, "Now what would make you think that?"

"If I began to explain, you may think we're crazy."

"Try me, Sam. I'm a fairly believing kind of guy." Sam took a sip of his drink and then began, "Well, Mount Elbert was apparently a resting place for wyverns, as well as a former hideout for the ones that stopped the clan. Not sure how much you know on the whole history, but we believe it is truer than just legend." John nodded his head, his face now growing serious. "I'm aware of the Dracosapiens and wyverns, yes. And how apparently the leopard shifting magic was rumored to have been sealed on the mountain." It was the group's turn to look surprised.

"Then would you believe us if we told you that the shifters walk again?" Sam delicately asked, not sure on how John would react. John looked around the restaurant and made sure no other patrons were within earshot. He then knelt at the table with a serious expression to begin speaking. "As much as I know the wyverns to be back again."

"You know of the Wyverns?" Sam asked, his curiosity piqued.

"I do. I have ties to them as one of the descendants of the Dracosapiens."

"You also do as well?" Sara asked, bewildered.

"Yes. When you first got hired on here, I was curious about your last name and the increased strange activity around here. I was seeing wyverns more, rumors of leopard sightings were going around, and the fact that Mount Elbert lit up like a searchlight beam into the sky last year cued me in. Your grandfather came in one night a few months ago and began to speak of the shifters again, trying to make jest. It was then we both realized we have a long-standing connection between our bloodlines."

"You did?! Then why didn't you say anything sooner?! What is this connection?!"

"Because Ed kept me informed of the events going on, and that we had shifters here. I wanted to lay low and observe from the shadows, to gather my own info to help your family and you guys. I'm sorry I didn't say anything sooner, but Ed has told me the situation at hand, and I can no longer stay quiet on the matter. Who do you think this establishment was named for?" Sara thought hard on the question but shrugged when she couldn't think of an answer. "My family comes from the line of Sir Ricard Vel, the leader of the Dracosapiens. I am his descendant." Sam and Sara's eyes nearly popped out of their heads, with the others taken aback by such a revelation. John smiled and replied,

"That's right. SRV Steakhouse: the calling card of a Dracosapiens member hidden in plain sight. I have ties to the wyverns, keeping in contact with them and maintaining relationships. I had spoken with one months ago on checking out Mount Elbert, and gave him a lead on doing so."

"You mean Loxa?" Sam asked.

"You know him?!" John asked excitedly.

"Yes! He and the other wyverns are currently looking for the shifter leader!"

"Then if all is true, that means you are one of the shifters as well. Though I understand you seek to stop them, which I fully support."

"Does this mean you have the ability to speak with the wyverns at will?"

"In a sense. I have a wyrm whistle that has been in the family for generations. It whistles a pitch so high and powerful; wyverns can hear it. If that is the case with you and Loxa, then we may all come together yet to bring the pieces together. Tell me, Sam, what is the full situation?"

"Okay, bear with me. Long story short, Rodrigo is back. He is teamed up with another essence user, and has begun making new ones. There's a hideout they have somewhere, which we have yet to discover, and which the wyverns are working on. Not only that, but the Sigma Pi members have been kidnapped as well. I don't know how he's making more essence users, but it's likely he's recreating the Jan Damis on a smaller scale. We cannot let him do such, or things could fall to chaos once again like they did." John's face went wide as he choked out in a hoarse whisper, "The Sigma Pi fellas are kidnapped?"

"Unfortunately," Sam nodded slowly, his face one of worry. "I tried to stop one of their top guys but failed to do so. In turn, they were all taken. The good news? I have help right here. Both Diego and Fiona here are also two of the six original essence users. The last? Fred here."

"Fred?! Really?! How did this happen?!"

"Remember Bradley and how he was arrested? He was an essence user until I stopped him and sealed away his power. We recently bestowed it to Fred to help in the upcoming conflict."

"Wow…that's a lot to take in," John mumbled. "But if that's the case, then seems like you have a good chance to get them back."

"That's the plan."

"Well then," John said as he stood up and smiled, "I would be honored to help you out in any way I can. You're not alone in this."

"We appreciate that, John," Sam responded, a smile on his face. "Helps to have allies, especially with so few of us against untold numbers of them." A ring with a purple gem began to glow on John's right finger, as the group looked to the strange light. "Ah, they're near," John replied.

"Who is they?" Sam asked.

"The wyverns. This is an enchanted ring that lets one know when wyverns are nearby. It was originally made by one of the Jan Damis from long ago, but the Dracosapiens took it and used it as a beacon for when their draconic allies were near. To this day, it still stands as just that."

"Will they show themselves here?" Sam asked. "No. They are high up out of visibility right now. They are waiting for me to close shop so that we may speak without people nearby." A heavy clunking noise was heard outside of the entrance, which John proceeded to go check. He came back shortly after with a smile on his face and a piece of paper in his hand. "What was it?" Fred asked. "A letter from Loxa," John replied. "It reads that they have found many shifters in one locale, pressured one into talking, and now have a general location of where they're based out of. Even better news for Loxa, as you'll be here to talk with him as well." Sam's eyes lit up with hope as the group exchanged excited glances. "I suppose we'll have a rescue to execute yet, Sam," Diego said to him. "Yes indeed, we will. Let us go have a word with Loxa later," Sam replied, feeling his spirits rise again. "We have a fraternity to rescue.